The Lord
AND THE WALLFLOWER

The Culpepper Misses, Book Three

COLLETTE CAMERON

Blue Rose Romance®

Sweet-to-Spicy Timeless Romance®

"No matter what the future held,

whether their paths intertwined or separated,

Brette would forever be branded upon his heart."

"Addictive and deliciously romantic--

Cameron's stories are a must-read!"

~Lauren Smith- USA Today Bestingselling Author

Other Collette Cameron Books

The Culpepper Misses
The Earl and the Spinster
The Marquis and the Vixen
The Lord and the Wallflower
The Buccaneer and the Bluestocking
The Lieutenant and the Lady

Check out Collette's Other Series
Castle Brides
Highland Heather Romancing a Scot
Daughters of Desire (Scandalous Ladies)
The Honorable Rogues®
Seductive Scoundrels
Heart of a Scot

Collections
Lords in Love
Heart of a Scot Books 1-3
The Honorable Rogues® Books 1-3
The Honorable Rogues® Books 4-6
Seductive Scoundrels Books 1-3
Seductive Scoundrels Books 4-6
The Culpepper Misses Books 1-2

Dedication

For my Beta Babes.

You know who you are, my dears!

Thank you for your time, your honest input, and your

insightful suggestions!

Acknowledgements

First and foremost, I have to thank my virtual assistant Cindy Jackson for her profound patience, attention to detail, and efficiency. She keeps me sane! And she does a fabulous job formatting my books, including ***The Lord and the Wallflower***. Lauren Smith gets a shout out for her fabulous cover quote. As always, the input from my Beta Babes and my ARC review team has been enormously helpful. Thank you from the bottom of my heart!

xoxo

Collette

An insightful woman acknowledges that every person receives their due according to what they've intended.
~*Appearances and Attitude—The Genteel Lady's Guide to Practical Living*

Bristledale Court
The English Countryside
Late August 1822

Brette Culpepper peeked around the carved door case, her stomach flipping in excitement.

Yes.

Engrossed in the objects before him, Lord Danfield hadn't a clue he'd played straight into her and Ophelia Thurston's plans.

Absolutely perfect.

Jolly good fun, this.

Bent at the waist, his expression one of awed concentration, the viscount closely examined the carved jadeite and white nephrite collection displayed beneath the glass covering.

Just as Brette had intended.

Well, more aptly, she'd hoped he couldn't resist the temptation. After she'd learned of his fascination with the foreign trinkets during supper last night, she'd broadly hinted at the vast assortment housed in Bristledale's library.

A library conveniently situated on the opposite side of the manor from where dignified footmen roamed scorching rooms, offering cooled champagne to overheated guests.

Brows furrowed, Lord Danfield lifted his head and stared outside through the open French windows, murmuring something while grazing his fingers along his jawline. Moonlight lit the veranda beyond, and a scant summer breeze carried a fountain's lyrical burbling into the house.

Even from her position by the door, Brette caught a faint whiff of jasmine.

No surprise the rather bashful lord had escaped this evening's noisy throng and made his way to the figurines. Wise move on his part. He'd been spared Major Wilkerson's exuberant vocal rendition. Lowing cattle claimed more musical aptitude than the jovial officer.

More than one disconcerted guest had emptied their champagne flute in a single swift pull before eagerly seizing another, as if hoping to mute the effects of the next amateur performer. If those presentations were anything like Major Wilkerson's, several more glasses of champagne might be in order before the entertainment recommenced.

"Utterly fascinating." Lord Danfield leaned nearer the case, paying particular attention to the more risqué carvings arranged along the back row. His red-tinged ears glowed noticeably; a close match for the shot of fiery hair topping his head.

To smother an undignified laugh, Brette clamped her teeth together. She, too, had blushed scarlet the first time she'd gazed upon the more scandalous statuettes. Tristin, the Marquis of Leventhorpe, their host and her cousin-in-law, possessed several such sculptures, which Lord Danfield seemed determined to commit to memory.

Down to every last naughty detail.

Danfield glanced toward the entrance for an instant, and Brette ducked behind the doorframe.

Had he heard her? Seen her?

She turned and, waving her hand, beckoned Ophelia.

The sable-haired beauty hovered near a curtained window, darting anxious glances up and down the corridor's length. As arranged earlier, they'd left the others on the pretense of needing to visit the ladies' retiring room during the musical intermission. After seeking Mrs. Thurston's permission, of course.

Ophelia's mama had nodded distractedly, a pinched look upon her lightly powdered face.

Apparently, after sitting through the major's vigorous performance, she'd needed a few moments' reprieve to collect herself. Next time, she might consider stuffing a scrap of cloth in her ears as Brette intended to.

Ophelia, her frilly ivory and rose pink skirts swishing in her haste, whisked to Brette's side.

She fiddled with her fan's lacy edge. "Danfield's inside? Alone?"

"He is, indeed." Brette's tummy gave another giddy quiver.

She adored this part—bringing star-crossed sweethearts together. So romantic and daring.

Like a story from a gothic novel except without all the drama and gloom.

Her fifth matchmaking jaunt since entering society, and so far, three rousing successes. The fourth—

She grimaced, the spasm in her middle caused by sick remorse rather than glee.

That had been a colossal disaster. So much so, she'd briefly considered forfeiting her newly self-appointed profession as Cupid's assistant. And she'd been having so much fun, too. Plus, the meddling—*no, no, I'm helping people*—gave her a purpose.

By Jove. This time would be different. She'd made sure of it.

Unlike her last unpleasant matchmaking escapade, Brette had investigated this moon-eyed pair thoroughly, and nary a scolding wife or piqued betrothed would caper along to interrupt her plan.

It honestly hadn't occurred to her that either person mightn't have been honorable in asking her to arrange a tryst. The ways of the upper ten thousand continued to baffle and frequently appall her. Fairly new to elite circles, she wasn't familiar with many *haut ton* members' connections, and she'd blundered by arranging for an affianced widower to meet with a humble, but sweet, newly-come-into-her-vulgarly-large-inheritance debutante.

If it hadn't been for Rector Alexander Hawksworth—Alex in her most private of thoughts— happening upon Brette as she'd opened the conservatory's door to permit Miss Marshall her rendezvous... A slight shudder rippled across Brette's shoulders, raising the hairs at her nape to rigid attention. *Gads.* She swallowed and pressed her palm to her stomach. The notion didn't bear pondering for long, or the dainties she'd nibbled earlier might sour in her stomach.

The rector had averted a monumental disaster when, less than a minute later, the widower's betrothed—the influential Lady Covington—famous for her swift temper, cutting tongue, and unforgiving nature had sailed their way.

"Given your humble origins, Miss Culpepper, you'd do well to apply your energies to acquiring a measure of decorum and social acceptance." Superior nose elevated and tone condescending, Lady Covington had flounced away. Stern disapproval had lined her lovely, but haughty, face as she towed her philandering, a-decade-her-junior intended to the ballroom, giving him an earful as they went.

The incident haunted Brette still.

Not only would Miss Marshall have been ruined, so, too, would Brette's family. Lady Covington, on intimate terms with a number of Almack's peeresses, would've seen them yanked from Society's loftiest perch and tossed into London's festering gutters. Never mind that Brette claimed a marquis and an earl as kin now. A featherless duck would've gained entrance to an assembly before the Culpeppers ever set a foot inside an elite parlor or drawing room again.

And unlike her sister and cousins, Brette adored the

social whirlwind, though she diligently kept that secret to herself. Preferring the country's serenity to Town's chaos, her family would have been nonplussed, at the least, and disapproving, at worst, if they'd known of her fascination with metropolitan life. They probably wouldn't have objected an iota if Lady Covington succeeded in having them blackballed.

According to Alex, Lady Covington was most unforgiving, and her betrothed, Phillip Lapley, a notorious womanizer. In order to get his hands on Miss Marshal's fortune, he'd have compromised the girl to force her into marriage.

Swine.

Shaken to her core, for two weeks afterward, Brette diligently refrained from all forms of plotting whatsoever. Except in her mind, of course. No harm in fantasizing and matchmaking there. Oh, she'd merrily united several woebegone wretches in the private alcoves of her imagination. But there the lovesick couples stayed, forever doomed to worshipping from afar, no one the wiser, save she.

Until, at another house party, she'd spotted Ophelia lurking within a curtained nook, peering dreamily at Lord Danfield as he spoke to Mr. Waters, a kindly merchant. Earlier that same day, Brette had stumbled upon the viscount loitering behind the shrubbery in the gardens near a secluded gazebo. An expression of moon-eyed adoration had wreathed his face as Ophelia and her brothers passed by.

If ever two people were destined to make a smashing match, Ophelia Thurston and Patrick, Viscount Danfield were. A shame if they should miss their chance at happiness, especially since Brette possessed the means to bring them together.

How could she have said no when Ophelia, wringing her hands, her doe-like eyes glimmering with tears, confessed her undying love for Lord Danfield? She'd begged Brette to arrange an assignation. Nothing too scandalous, of course. Simply a short, respectable few moments to speak together without Mrs. Thurston's eagle eye watching her daughter's every move.

However had Ophelia learned of Brette's hush-hush hobby? Surprised, but pleased, Brette had nudged Alex's warning into a remote corner of her mind, hidden it beneath a blanket of good intentions, and eagerly agreed to help.

"He's inside, waiting," Brette whispered with another harried glance along the corridor's length.

Not waiting, precisely, but he'd welcome Ophelia's unexpected appearance. No doubt about that.

Brette would allow them five minutes, discreetly hovering outside the open door for propriety's sake.

Afterward, she'd escort the enraptured young woman to her protective mother's side. Mrs. Thurston seldom permitted Ophelia out of her sight unless in the company of her trio of brothers. The moment must be seized. Another mightn't come along anytime soon.

A lilting whistle carried to them, and Brette and Ophelia exchanged troubled glances before peering into the passageway.

Botheration. Someone approached.

Probably Alex Hawksworth. Worse than a songbird with his perpetual, cheerful warbling, but my, could he sing. Even better than he whistled, which said something.

Why hadn't he been impressed upon to entertain this evening?

Now *that* Brette would've enjoyed. He possessed a lovely baritone, and many a lady, from aged dowagers to knobby-kneed girls fresh from the schoolroom, sighed rapturously when he sang. Or spoke. Or walked into the room—all masculine grace, power, and beauty.

And when he smiled— Lord help the woman he directed that devastating flash of teeth toward. Including her. Come to think of it, she responded in the most peculiar fashion whenever he drew near. Most disconcerting.

His appearance right now, however, was a major

inconvenience. He'd disapprove of her interfering. The last time, he'd scolded her, kindly but soundly.

"No matter how well-intended you might've been, Miss Culpepper," he'd insisted with a look not quite patronizing but not benevolent either, "when it comes to matters of the heart, people should let Nature take her course."

Showed how little he knew of love. Obviously, he'd never experienced the emotion.

She hadn't either, but she'd read several novels on the subject. Besides, it didn't take someone with extensive practice to realize that people, afraid of making a mistake or looking an unrequited fool, needed a slight prod in the right direction. Particularly if they'd each confessed their tendre to a mutual third party. Say, a well-meaning miss, fresh from the country with too much time on her hands and too little to do.

"Hurry, Ophelia." Brette gripped Ophelia's elbow, tossing a frantic glance toward the muted chatter and laughter filtering to them from the other guests. They'd be missed soon, if they hadn't been already. "You've only a minute or two now before we must return."

In the midst of a fancy trill, the whistling ended abruptly.

Blast me.

Alex had spotted them.

Brette dug her nails into the woodwork. He'd ruin everything she'd worked so hard to organize. Did he think it easy to arrange these stolen moments for others?

She wrinkled her nose. For pity's sake. Unmarried women were guarded more closely than the king's treasury.

What could possibly happen in five little minutes?

Naturally, his position required his disapproval of romantic ventures, but surely even he, pledged to uphold morality and abstinence from fleshly corruption, possessed an amorous speck beneath his stark and entirely proper clothing. *Poise and prim all the time.* For a handsome man, he was positively stuffy.

Unfair.

Her conscience gave her a disappointed jab. Not true. Not at all, actually. Mayhap she merely wished it, to make him less appealing.

He possessed a delightful sense of humor, and she'd never have guessed he was a man of the cloth when they'd first met. In fact, he'd been so charming and grand, his looks so arresting and charismatic, her cousin, Blaire, had assumed him an actor or opera singer, despite his somber togs.

Brette mistook him for a valet.

Until he spoke, and the notion dissolved as rapidly as finely ground spice in stew. With his angular cheeks, full lips, and strong jaw, he would've been brilliant on the stage and amassed a following in short order.

As it was, his parish pews overflowed with enamored ladies, from dewy-eyed misses to dames long past their prime. Given the impossibly scanty bodices Brette observed on Sundays, a sermon on modesty wouldn't have gone amiss. Last week, if Miss Lacewell had sung any more exuberantly, Brette had truly feared that her bosoms would escape the straining fabric's confines, and the reverend would've had to preach with his eyes pinched closed.

"Too bad *he* cannot claim position or wealth." Attention glued to the golden-haired man strolling in their direction, Ophelia whispered in Brette's ear, her voice annoyingly breathy. "Mr. Hawksworth by far the handsomest man I've ever laid eyes upon. Godlike even, but pauper poor." She sighed theatrically. "Mama says I must marry a man with a title. She's determined it should be so. And I do favor Lord Danfield more than other lords."

And his wealth, too, I'll be bound.

"Money and station aren't everything." Brette sneaked the rector a sideway look. Alex was one of the most decent men she'd met since her sister, Brooke, married Heath, the Earl of Ravensdale.

Nonetheless, in the immoral and pretentious upper

circles, wealth and position ranked near the top. Pitiful, really. To place such importance on two criteria having nothing to do with a person's character and which could in no way guarantee happiness or contentment.

"Rather too bad, isn't it? An infinite waste of superb manhood." Ophelia sighed wistfully again. "He'll probably marry a mousy, plain-faced, flat-as-a-washboard-chested dowd who's memorized an annoying amount of scripture."

For someone madly in love with the viscount, she sounded most inappropriately enraptured.

Her pink tongue trailed her lower lip as her gaze trailed to Alex's groin.

Hmm. And not as innocent as her big, rich caramel eyes and virginal gown suggested.

"Ah, Miss Culpepper. Miss Thurston." Alex strode toward them, his fair brow cocked meaningfully and a barely restrained smile twitching his mouth's corners. "Your mother inquires after you, Miss Thurston. I told her I thought I'd last seen you in the corridor outside the peach parlor. I'm sure that's where you're away to now, isn't it? No one lurked about when I passed moments ago. You should escape notice if you hurry along."

Ophelia formed her rosy bowed mouth into a moue, and after an extended, regretful glance at the cracked doorway, tossed her glossy chestnut curls and flounced off in the direction she'd come.

Brette pressed her forefinger to her upper lip and shook her head once. Had she misjudged Ophelia's interest in Lord Danfield? Did his title and wealth enchant her, rather than any true affection? Surely not.

Alex joined Brette at the door and toed it open another inch.

Danfield had gravitated to the case's other side and now faced the door, though his attention remained riveted on the knickknacks.

My, he certainly seemed intent on satisfying his curiosity.

Alex drew her away and bent near her ear—a considerable distance since her head barely reached his shoulder. Of the five Culpepper misses—well, two were married now—she alone possessed a petite stature and greenish tinted eyes. She assumed she resembled a forgotten ancestor.

"Danfield's rather a lackluster sort," Alex whispered as if an authority on the chap. "Always has his nose in a fusty tome and would rather study ancient specimens than flirt with young, empty-headed misses."

Brette glanced upward, almost returning his infectious grin. Almost. She mightn't be terribly miffed, but he wouldn't be forgiven just like that either.

He boasted the most mesmerizing eyes, a

spectacular green, like newly sprouted spring grass. Bright, cheery, and framed by honey-tipped lashes so lush, they appeared coffee-brown from a distance. He smelled wonderful too. Sandalwood, starch, and a woodsy, soapy smell. Clean and fresh. Quite irresistible. If she were the type to be taken with such, which, being a practical sort, she was not.

His gaze, oddly mesmerizing, held hers and for an instant, she quite forgot her purpose for being in the passage.

"Particularly flighty, title-hunting ninnies," Alex said.

What? Oh, he meant Ophelia.

True, Ophelia was flighty, and she did seek a titled husband, but if she were enamored with the gentleman, surely that made all the difference.

Careful to keep her voice subdued, Brette murmured, "Shows what you know, Al—Mr. Hawksworth." *Blast me twice.* Did he notice her blunder?

"I've asked you, repeatedly, to call me Alex or Hawk."

Yes, he had. Heat crept from her neck to her hairline, and she snapped her fan open, welcoming the faint breeze.

His smile widened, crinkling the corner of his eyes

in a merry manner. He sniffed lightly. "I like your perfume. Is it new?" He bent near her again and boldly smelled her hair.

Such an intimate, improper thing to dare.

Brette's jaw hung slack momentarily before she collected herself. Hadn't she just been thinking how pleasant he smelled? It rather disconcerted her to have his mind marching along the same path as hers.

He flashed another disarming smile, and her stomach's renewed flopping had nothing to do with her matchmaking exploits. She fanned herself faster.

Did Alex's smile expand the merest iota more? As if he knew caterpillars, and butterflies, and all sort of ill-mannered insects cavorted about in her middle?

"Gentleman do not sniff ladies' heads, Mr. Hawksworth." What she'd intended as a sternly whispered reprimand came out as an amused observation. Nevertheless, reminding him of his position should put him in his place nicely.

"They do when they smell as lovely as you, and since you've forgotten again, I'll remind you that I've asked you to address me as Hawk or Alex." His melodic whisper held not a jot of repentance.

He most assuredly wasn't cut from the typical clerical cloth.

She'd never noticed the citrine flecks rimming his

pupils before. When he was amused, they danced, and he definitely found something funny right now. Her.

Folding her fan, she considered him. Should she be flattered or annoyed?

"That's too familiar, even if you are one of my brother-in-law's dearest friends."

She canted her head toward Lord Danfield, still absorbed in the treasure trove. "Besides, he and Miss Thurston have a tendre for each other. They may not seem well-suited, but that doesn't mean they couldn't be happy together. Who has the right to decide except them?"

Cupping her elbow, his hands surprisingly strong for a cleric, Alex guided her away from the library. An accomplished pugilist, he practiced at least twice weekly, Heath had mentioned once in passing. That probably accounted for Alex's robust grip on her arm. With his parish responsibilities, when did he find the time to spar?

Come to think of it, how had he managed to escape his duties for this house party?

Of much more importance, could she possibly arrange another tryst for Danfield and Ophelia? Brette pivoted halfway around to consider Danfield.

He'd disappeared.

Poor decisions are still poor decisions,
no matter how grand, kind, or gallant the intention.
*~Appearances and Attitude—The Genteel Lady's
Guide to Practical Living*

2

B rette breathed a relieved sigh.

Thank goodness, Danfield chose to exit through the French windows and not the door. Awkward, having to explain why she and Alex skulked outside the library, whispering like impish schoolgirls.

"I thought, given that disastrous incident with Lady Covington, you'd ceased your matchmaking antics, Brette. I'm not persuaded she's forgiven you yet." Alex peered at her, humor and genuine concern brimming in his eyes.

"Oh, pooh. That was ages ago." She shook her closed fan at him. "And I did her a favor, revealing Lapley's libertine character." Though Brette didn't have the impression Lady Covington simmered with gratitude or had been ignorant of her sweetheart's flaws.

Alex propelled Brette along as if demons nipped at

their heels. "Want to know what I think?"

"No, not particularly." Brette slanted a brow as she lifted her skirt higher to keep pace with his lengthy strides. Why didn't he mind his own business and stop interfering with hers?

His lips twitched. "I'll tell you anyway. I think you're bored and need a project."

Spot on, there.

"Something worthwhile to satisfy your need to feel useful." He nodded once and directed his attention to the detailed crown molding. "You're accustomed to busyness, and if I may be candid?" He didn't wait for her to agree. "These house parties can be dull as cheap paper at times."

"*You* think so too?" Grinning, she stopped in her tracks. Delighted, she forgave him his boldness in addressing her by her given name and his presumptuousness for interfering too.

Though many deemed the country life of the social elite quaint, Brette found it tediously turtle-paced and eye-crossingly boring. Quite impolite to harbor those uncharitable views, but how many card games, strolls across the green, or sipping of cups and *cups* of tea could one endure?

Or caterwauling passing as singing?

So help her God, if she played one more game of

croquet, charades, or shuttlecock, she'd scream.

"Indeed. I dozed off during tea today with no one the wiser." Alex chuckled, that contagious rumble that made her laugh too. "That is, until I released a minute— I'm positive it was quite inconspicuous—snore."

"You snored? During tea?" Shaking her head, she giggled while picturing him dozing, chin slack, over his delicate china cup and biscuits.

"So Lady Ravensdale informed me, after none-too-gently elbowing me awake."

"I should've liked to have seen that." Brette had missed tea today. Intentionally. If forced to tolerate another discussion about the weather, flora, or whom had just become betrothed to whom, she'd begin nipping Leventhorpe's excellent sherry.

Her hand resting on Alex's arm, they entered the ballroom turned recital area. Instead of steering Brette to the neat rows of chairs again filling with guests for the musicale's second half, he directed her toward the makeshift stage.

Mrs. Thurston and her stern-faced husband stood beside the second row, craning their necks this way and that, no doubt looking for Ophelia. She must have made use of the ladies' retiring room after all. Ophelia qualified as a first-rate flibbertigibbet, but she was kind and, occasionally, even thoughtful.

While subtly trying to extract her arm from Alex's grasp, Brette smiled at her cousin, Blythe, the new Lady Leventhorpe. Blythe chatted with her sisters, Blaire and Blaike.

More than one confused houseguest had commented on the oddity of the sisters and cousins having names beginning with B. Even Brette had to admit how perplexing it must be to those newly acquainted with the Culpeppers. The girls had determined amongst themselves that the tradition of females receiving names beginning with B would end with their generation.

Alex canted his head in response to Captain Whitehouse's and Lieutenant Drake's brief greetings as he and Brette made their way past the blond trio. "Come along, Brette."

Obstinate man. He must leave off addressing her so familiarly. People might get the wrong impression about them.

"What are you doing?" Whispering from the side of her mouth, Brette scanned the room and subtly tried maneuvering her arm free.

Alex urged her forward, but no one seemed to pay them much mind. "I don't sing, Alex. Really, I don't. I can barely carry a tune."

Panic welled. She wasn't exaggerating.

She neither sang nor played an instrument for public spectacle, and for good reason. 'Twas a cruel crime against humankind. Compared to her, Major Wilkerson was a gifted vocalist. Her talents lay in baking, sewing, crocheting, and painting. And dancing.

She loved to dance. Especially the notorious waltz. Such grace and flowing movement, and the music...? Utterly entrancing.

Alex's mouth twisted into his ever-ready and oh-so-charming grin. "Weren't you aware?

I'm scheduled to entertain next. I rather like the stage. Wanted to be an actor or a dance master in my youth, truth to tell. Naturally, the misplaced notion was quashed. Not respectable, you know."

Brette easily imagined him upon the stage. Perhaps his experience behind the pulpit lent him the confidence to perform in front of others. An aptitude she didn't share.

"And what does that have to do with me?" Suspicion danced along the column of her spine, and not a delicate, graceful step. More of a heavy-footed stamping. He must be made to understand. They couldn't sing a duet.

Brette was tone deaf. Utterly. Profoundly.

"But, I must have a Heloise to direct my prose too." He gave a flourishing half-bow, enjoying this far more than he ought. "Abelard at your service."

Who the devil are they?

Alex waggled his dark, honey-blond eyebrows and sighed melodramatically. "Such a poignant tale of star-crossed lovers."

She started. Faith, he'd read her mind.

Shaking her head, Brette resisted his gentle onward tug. Unobtrusively, of course. Wouldn't do to draw attention. "I haven't a clue who Heloise or Abelard are, but I'm not going to play her. Unlike you, I'm not accustomed to the masses staring at me."

Blaire fluttered her fingertips in their direction, and Brette summoned a sunny smile and waved in return.

Besides, wouldn't people read something into his selecting her to stand opposite him? *Le beau monde* needed no help contriving juicy *on dit* to bandy about, even if those present tonight were mostly Lord Leventhorpe's intimates. The exception being the Thurstons, his nearest neighbors.

Alex had managed to maneuver Brette to the stage's edge, the sly devil. Unless she made a scene, her fate seemed sealed. Did he think she wouldn't kick up a dust? Not the kind he'd expect. She raised a hand to her forehead, prepared to crumple into a swoon.

Never mind that she hadn't succumbed to the vapors in her life. She'd make the sacrifice to spare the guests a far worse fate than a little concerned *tsking* and tutting.

"Romantic that you are, Brette, you'll like their slightly gothic story. Though I fear their tale ends rather sadly."

She lowered her hand. Perhaps she needn't throw herself on the floor after all.

"They do marry and have a child— unfortunately, not in that order. Which is why her uncle, a diabolical chap, separates them and has Abelard castrated. Poor Albelard becomes a monk, and his beloved Heloise, a nun. They never see each other again."

"That's awful, Alex. Why would you want to share that heartrending account? In love and forced apart? Tragic, if you ask me." She gave her arm another tug, and he released her this time, his attention focused above her head.

His eyebrows shrugged together before his troubled gaze sank to hers. "Brette?"

Apprehension contracted her muscles from hip to shoulder.

Confound it. Now what?

"Miss Culpepper?" Worry permeated Mrs. Thurston's voice high-pitched voice. "Where's my dear Ophelia?"

Brette twisted as Mrs. Thurston descended on her

like a general taking to the battlefield, while Mr. Thurston, his countenance grave, spoke to a footman by the ballroom entrance.

His wife's anxious gaze flitted about the room before coming to rest accusingly on Brette.

"I'm sure she'll be along shortly, Mrs. Thurston." No wonder Ophelia escaped her mother's domineering presence whenever possible.

"Don't tell me you left her unattended?" Mrs. Thurston's voice rose even higher, to a disbelieving squeak.

Egad. Such overreaction.

Brette hadn't left Ophelia alone in a brothel surrounded by drunken, pillaging pirates, for pity's sake.

"She was headed to the peach parlor the last time I saw her, not more than ten minutes ago, but I suspect she made use of the retiring room as well." *And I hardly think she needed my assistance there.* Brette veered Alex a puzzled glance before giving Mrs. Thurston an encouraging, if somewhat forced, smile. "I've no doubt she'll be along momentarily."

She had better be.

"Eloped!" Mr. Thurston thundered, waving a piece of paper in the air as he stalked toward his wife. "My daughter's eloped with that twiddepoop Danfield."

"Devil take it," Alex muttered as the room grew tomb silent for a heart-stopping instant before a symphony of whispers started slowly and grew into an ever-increasing frenzy.

Bully for Danfield, though. Didn't think the chap had it in him.

Alex couldn't help but admire the viscount for acquiring mettle at last and daring to cock a snook at propriety. He didn't dare voice his admiration, though. Rectors mustn't condone brash behavior, even if they secretly admired the gumption. But in this case, Alex feared Danfield had made a major misjudgment in choosing the capricious Miss Thurston as his bride.

"Oh, how could she do this to me?" One eye cracked a slit, Mrs. Thurston flung a hand to her chest, her actions suspiciously rehearsed. Her face a mask of motherly anguish, her other arm extended palm upward, she swayed.

Definitely rehearsed.

"Foolish girl. If she'd waited, he'd have offered for her. I'm sure of it." Pale, but composed, Brette steadied Mrs. Thurston. Casting a hurried glance 'round the captivated onlookers, she bit her lower lip.

Anger skewed Thurston's already gloomy countenance. "They're probably halfway to Gretna Green by now. No thanks to you, gel."

"Not in ten minutes, they aren't," Brette countered. "I'll be bound they haven't left Bristledale Court's lands yet."

She made a valid point.

By George, Thurston should've used discretion. Now the chance to salvage his daughter's reputation was slimmer than Satan waltzing in heaven. Surely the codshead realized broadcasting the elopement sealed Miss Thurston's fate. And if Alex wasn't mistaken, the gleam in Mrs. Thurston's eyes resembled cat-like satisfaction rather than genuine motherly distress.

He narrowed his gaze, studying first her calculated distress before scrutinizing her husband's blustering.

Something didn't ring true here.

Mayhap the Thurstons weren't as dismayed as they appeared at this disastrous turn of events.

"I lay the blame directly at your feet, Miss Culpepper. You should've stayed with Ophelia," Mrs. Thurston accused, her faced pinched into bitter lines.

What, and hold her hand as she attended to her personal needs?

"Let's gather the facts before jumping to

conclusions." Leventhorpe wound through the guests, murmuring reassurances.

Astute chap. He'd immediately assessed the situation.

"Let's retire to my study where we can discuss this privately." He beckoned to Lady Leventhorpe. "My dear, would you please sing for our guests in Hawk's stead? And perhaps you can play the piano and our company might also enjoy impromptu dancing?"

Anything to keep the houseguests occupied. Her ladyship possessed extraordinary talent, and the sooner the visitors were distracted, the better.

Lady Leventhorpe bowed her neck. "Of course."

Ravensdale and his lady, Brooke, joined Brette.

"I'll accompany you to the study," Raven offered. "But, we'll need riders to intercept Danfield as soon as possible. Drake and Whitehouse, will you attend to readying the horses?"

"At once," Drake agreed, and after an abbreviated bow, he and Whitehouse departed.

Likely they, along with Raven and Leventhorpe, would give chase, while Alex, as usual, would be obliged to stay behind and comfort Miss Thurston's fretting parents. He would've much preferred to tear across the country, neck or nothing, with the others.

Minutes later, Brette perched serenely on the toast-colored leather sofa's crackling edge.

However, her clenched hands and the occasional flexing of her delicate jaw revealed her agitation. Her determined chin inched upward as she blew out a breath, causing the wispy flaxen strands framing her face to poof upward.

She was an extraordinarily beautiful woman, and the candles' glow caught the platinum riches of her glorious hair and emphasized her smooth, honeyed skin. In the flattering light, everything about her gleamed feminine and petal-soft.

Was her skin truly so smooth? He longed to find out, to explore the satiny contours. Impossible.

Her beauty never failed to impact him thus. He could stare at her, a true and rare incomparable, for hours. Like a perfectly painted portrait. Yet, she couldn't become aware of his fascination.

He'd deduced her love of Town excitement, and his position didn't pay enough to maintain the opulent lifestyle she'd been introduced to. He attended the various soirées and routs as his chums' guest. Their hospitality also provided him with rooms and meals when he visited, else he'd not have been able to rub elbows with the *ton*'s denizens at all.

At times, he rather resembled a parasite, taking advantage of his hosts and those he held dearest. No matter how many times Raven and Leventhorpe assured him such wasn't the case, guilt niggled, poking at Alex's conscience.

He was a man of God now.

He shouldn't crave the opera or theater. Shouldn't anticipate the balls and musicals, the hectic pace of the social set during the Season. Nevertheless, he did, and sacrificing his favorite activities when he'd been obliged to accept his appointment as rector had him tippled for a week.

Ruminating won't change things. Control your thoughts and attend to the matter at hand.

The Marquis of Leventhorpe rubbed his chin, his calm regard shifting from the overwrought Thurstons to Brette. "Remind us again when you last saw Miss Thurston."

"As I explained, we parted in the corridor outside the library. Ophelia indicated she intended to stop in the parlor." Normally, Brette was unflappable, but her turned-up nose and the saucy glint in her eye bespoke her annoyance at being blamed for Miss Thurston's rashness.

Miss Thurston had led many a man on a merry chase before this. Nonetheless, if Brette hadn't been matchmaking again—

Leventhorpe's brows knitted. "Why were you

outside the library?"

"Precisely what I'd like to know." Hands clasped behind his back, Thurston paced behind the sofa, exchanging telling looks with his wife every few moments.

Alex may not have wanted to be St. Peter's rector, but he possessed an uncanny ability to read people and persuade them to tell the truth. And, by Jove, the Thurstons lied through their less-than-well-cared-for teeth.

Brette's clear gaze met each of the room's occupants in turn. She angled her elegant chin again, and Alex's admiration grew. She wasn't cowed. Why should she be? She'd acted out of the misplaced goodness of her heart.

He passed his hand over his mouth to hide a budding smile before someone detected his fascination with her.

"I'm waiting for an explanation as to why my daughter didn't go directly to the retiring room." Thurston puffed out his chest and cheeks, his side whiskers dancing beside his fleshy face like giant, writhing caterpillars.

Brette folded her hands in her lap. "I arranged for Ophelia to encounter his lordship in the library, which I realize now was imprudent."

"I should say it was." Mrs. Thurston waved her fan before her flushed face, condemnation shooting from her eyes.

"Please allow her to finish, Mrs. Thurston." Leventhorpe flicked his forefinger. "Go on, Brette."

"I assumed if I acted as their chaperone, a few moments together would be harmless."

Brette's attention swept to Alex for the briefest instant, the faintest whisper of a glance, and he gave her an encouraging partial wink. "Mr. Hawksworth came upon us, and Ophelia left without speaking to Lord Danfield or him being aware we waited outside the library."

Except Danfield had known.

Alex had made eye contact with him and received a rather cheeky grin in response.

"You overstepped the bounds, Miss Culpepper. We entrusted our daughter to your care, and you betrayed our trust." Thurston shook his finger at her before facing Ravensdale. "Your ward is responsible for my daughter's ruination. What do you mean to do about it? You should permanently banish her to the countryside. That should put an end to her meddling. And be aware, I may seek damages in court."

His rampage lacked real conviction. Wouldn't a frantic father rush after his wayward child rather than linger in the study spouting accusations? A parent truly distraught would've done so immediately, and that he didn't roused misgivings.

"Don't fault Lord Ravensdale, Mr. Thurston. I presumed too much and am solely responsible for what's occurred." Brette met his infuriated glare unflinchingly. "I realize my folly in having trusted Ophelia. Pure foolishness on my part."

Mrs. Thurston huffed and spluttered. "You... you dare to blame my precious daughter?"

"Your precious daughter intentionally deceived Miss Culpepper and me, Mrs. Thurston."

Alex had warned Brette this might happen, yet he couldn't blame her entirely. She possessed a servant's heart and wanted people happy. Plus, if he wasn't sorely mistaken, she was more than a bit bored. Accustomed to hard work, few luxuries, and even less time for idleness, she needed something to occupy her and her time.

His parish sponsored a foundling home, and if he could acquire the funds, he wanted to establish a ragged school to offer London's street children a basic education. Surely she could find something to occupy her time at the home. Lord knew the pitiable children would benefit from the attention and love, and given the stern lines wrinkling Raven's forehead, she wouldn't escape this escapade without repercussions.

Alex would do his best to persuade Raven to allow Brette to work off her penance by volunteering at the foundling home or his church, though how he'd tolerate her regular presence without declaring himself, he didn't know.

Raven cupped his nape, giving Brette an assessing sidelong look. Lines of frustration framed his mouth and eyes. "Nonetheless, Brette, as your guardian, I am also responsible. We'll discuss this later, and I shall decide on the best course of action. At present, our main concern is setting out at once. Miss Thurston and Danfield have the advantage of a head start, but they cannot travel far at night by carriage, even with a full moon."

Raven brought this on himself when he married Brooke and assumed guardianship of her sister and cousins. Five diamonds of the first water had him running ragged.

Poor chap. Raven would be bald as a billiard ball and wrinkled as a crone by the time the last Culpepper married.

Alex almost laughed aloud.

Lady Ravensdale sat beside her sister and took her hand. "I know you meant well, Brette, but you acted recklessly. And truthfully, I'm surprised. It's not like you at all. You're sensible and steady." She angled her elegant head, contemplating the Thurstons. "We'll have ourselves a coze tomorrow and get to the bottom of what's really going on."

"I'll tell you what's going on." Thurston stopped his agitated stomping and gripped the sofa's back. "An upstart bumpkin has breached society's boundaries, and my daughter must pay the price."

His jowls shook with his agitation as he resumed his tramping back and forth. The carpet wouldn't be the same, given his tendency to scuff his feet as if lifting them proved too much of an effort. Considering the condition of his estate and person, his laziness wasn't altogether surprising.

Drawing back the weighty cerulean brocade draperies, Alex searched the drive. Several carriages stood at the ready, their coachmen clustered in a circle, chatting. These conveyances belonged to neighbors living close enough to make the moonlight trip to and from home. Had Miss Thurston's bags been hidden within their vehicle?

Her romantic flight had been planned; he hadn't a single doubt.

For parents whose daughter, at this very instant, gallivanted to Gretna Green, the Thurstons seemed remarkably unruffled. And Mrs. Thurston's uncharacteristic lack of tears throughout this ordeal had Alex narrowing his eyes in suspicion. Especially, since he'd seen evidence of her waterworks at the slightest provocation previously. Say, a tear in her hem, an undesirable seating arrangement at dinner, a perceived snub, or being denied the last seed cake slice when another guest selected the dainty first.

Alex dropped the drapery and, after straightening its folds, crossed his arms. "What's done is done. Lieutenant Drake and Captain Whitehouse rode out just now. If anyone can catch Danfield and Miss Thurston, they can."

"They rode out? Already? Without waiting for my direction?" Rather than appearing grateful, Thurston rapidly blinked his buggy eyes and clawed at his cravat.

"You don't approve, Thurston? I should think you'd be greatly relieved. Drake's a fine tracker. The best, truthfully." Alex fingered the thick, silk cord restraining the draperies.

A knock rattled the study door an instant before Chambers stepped into the room, leaving the door partially open behind him. Lady Leventhorpe's lovely singing voice carried into the study. *She* should have taken to the stage. Truly rare, a talent such as hers.

"I beg your pardon, my lord, but Miss Thurston is outside," Chambers announced. "I assumed you'd wish to see her at once."

Miss Thurston?

Another shock this evening. God spare them any more. Chambers pressed his lips together. "She's in a … froth."

She must be hysterical for Chambers to comment on her state.

"I must speak with my parents at once, Chambers. A most wretched mistake has been averted."

A well-bred woman keeps
this truth in the forefront of her mind:
Intentions are irrelevant if perceived the wrong way.
~*Appearances and Attitude—The Genteel Lady's
Guide to Practical Living*

3

Alex couldn't help the smug satisfaction sweeping him. Something about this whole deuced thing had been off from the start, and his qualms led him straight to the Thurstons.

Pushing Chambers aside, Miss Thurston stormed into the room, the Culpeppers' decrepit and poor-sighted Welsh corgi, Freddy, toddling in behind her.

"Ophelia? Whatever are you doing *here*?" Making an odd choking noise, Mrs. Thurston fluttered her hands near her chest and, blinking like a startled owl, veered her husband a stricken glance.

Brette's eyes narrowed until only her blue-green irises showed, an almost humorous contrast to her lips' sweet upward tilt. "You don't exactly appear overjoyed. I wonder why?"

Freddy snuffled his way to Brette and Lady Ravensdale. After giving their slippers a thorough sniffing, he tried to drag his portly self onto the sofa. His stubby legs worked frantically as he hopped and wriggled in vain.

Brette took pity on him and hoisted the pudgy dog onto a cushion, where he promptly collapsed, tail thumping and tongue lolling.

As a child, Alex had wanted a dog, but Mother refused, claiming his frail health wouldn't permit such a *filthy* beast. Later, without a place to call his own, he hadn't succumbed to the urge.

Freddy, his charcoal eyes shining, gazed up at Brette adoringly as she absently scratched behind his ears.

Mayhap Alex would find himself a stray pup and give it a home at the parish. He could certainly use the company. People wrongly assumed he either capered about nightly with his high-born chums or sought the entertainment ladies freely offered.

Far from the truth, that.

Most evenings found him preparing his sermon or dining with a parishioner, usually one with a marriageable daughter. He'd become skilled at maintaining a cordial smile while deflecting the girl's wayward hands groping his thighs beneath the tablecloth.

He *should* have been an actor.

Other nights, a book in hand and drowsy from boredom, he lounged before his smallish coal grate. Those times, loneliness gripped him the worst, and he'd welcome a furry friend's company.

"I couldn't do as you bid," Miss Thurston whined. *Spoilt, pampered child.* "I tried, Mama and Papa, I truly did."

Aha. I knew it.

A man of God oughtn't to be overjoyed at the revelation, but now Brette would be vindicated, and proving her innocence outweighed Alex's failings as a rector.

"But once in the coach," Miss Thurston rattled on, "when Danfield started blathering about our wedding trip. How he wanted to visit moldy Egyptian tombs and hot, dusty ruins. And then—if you can believe it, for I simply cannot—he dragged a musty volume on hiero ... hieroglumps or something as awful sounding and impossible to pronounce from his satchel."

"Hieroglyphs, perhaps?" Lady Ravensdale's shoulders trembled suspiciously as she allowed Freddy into her lap.

"I suppose so." Miss Thurston plopped into a chair, a mutinous pout upon her pretty face. "Well, I tell you,

I couldn't go through with the elopement. I couldn't bear a lifetime of that—of *him*. Not even for fifteen thousand annually."

Would she never cease?

Miss Thurston shuddered delicately. "He had the nerve to ask if I knew what a scarab was. He laughed when I suggested it might be a sort of gem. I don't think it too much to anticipate he'd have a trinket for me. Something to show his devotion."

Now Brette's shoulders shook too, and she coughed into her hand.

Her pert nose wrinkling in disgust, Miss Thurston pursed her lips. "But did he have a bauble for me? No, indeed." She stretched the word out, emphasizing her disgust. "He wanted to talk about nasty beetles, munching ... *pooh*. Pooh, of all the ridiculous twaddle. A mere ten minutes, and I wanted to toss Danfield from the carriage."

A distinct snort of laughter echoed from Leventhorpe's direction.

"But, my darling, your reputation's tarnished. You've no choice except to wed him." Mrs. Thurston, her face a peculiar shade between pea-green and ash, forced a brittle smile, the flinty glint in her eyes belying her loving words.

Thurston's perpetual scowl deepened until his eyes

became two puffy slices. He pounded the sofa's back. "I shall demand Danfield marry you. You've been compromised."

"Bah, what fribble. He didn't even kiss my fingers." Miss Thurston flapped her gloved hand back and forth. "I don't think the man has an interest in women, truth be known. Unless they've been dead a century or two. Then he's agog over their fusty bones."

Raven elbowing Leventhorpe in the ribs cut short the latter's guffaw.

Her father puffed out his strawberry red cheeks. "You will do as I say, young lady or—"

"I shan't do it." Miss Thurston crossed her arms, thrust her stubborn jaw upward, and glared at her parents. "*You* wanted Danfield's money and position. Would have me sacrifice myself for your benefit and comfort." Her focus slid to the windows, and her features softened. "Besides, I love another, and if he'll still have me, I intend to wed him."

Beneath his breath, Raven muttered to Leventhorpe. "Wonder who might *that* lucky chap be?"

Leventhorpe grinned, hunching a shoulder. "I cannot believe Danfield tried to discuss insects—*poop-eating insects*—while eloping. Only he would find such drivel romantic."

Brette's lips twitched and laughter danced in her

expressive eyes before she lowered her glossy head.

Alex yearned to run his fingers through those silky tresses.

"I'm of age, and I shan't be stopped." Miss Thurston speared her parents a mutinous look. "Mr. Waters is a decent man with an adequate income."

At her admission, Brette's head shot up, her mouth forming an O of surprise.

Hers wasn't the only jaw sagging. A pelican might have built a nest in Thurston's gaping mouth.

"Wat ... ters?" he stuttered, yanking at his cravat again and sounding like he'd chewed hot bricks. "The ... the *merchant*, Waters?"

Mrs. Thurston's mouth snapped shut with a loud pop as she collapsed against the sofa, eyes closed, agitatedly fanning her face. "Dear Lord," she moaned. "Our daughter shall smell of the shop. What will people say?"

Miss Thurston prattled on. "You can choose to support me in this. Or you can oppose me. Regardless, I shall marry Jerome, and you'll see neither me nor a single shilling from him either."

"But, darling," her mother objected.

She gave each of her shocked parents a flinty stare. "I mean it."

Alex feared Ophelia's parents would suffer an

apoplexy. Their faces mottled into the most astounding reddish-brown hue, and their mouths worked silently, rather like gasping bass on the shore.

Miss Thurston almost deserved applause.

He'd underestimated the chit. Misjudged her too. He understood her dismay at being forced into a position she didn't want because others deemed it suitable. Blasphemous for a cleric to think those thoughts. Shouldn't his conscience jab or poke or chastise a little? Or a lot?

True, he thought of himself as a Godly man and had enjoyed attending church even before becoming a rector. He didn't have horrendous vices, but he certainly wasn't a saint either. And most assuredly, he had no desire to shepherd a flock of clucking or grumbling ninnies for decades.

He'd rather teach dance or voice, truth to tell.

"You mean to tell me the three of you plotted this conundrum?" Brette stood, and her cobalt satin gown swished softly as she planted her hands on her slim hips. Outrage resonated in each clipped syllable as she pointed her finger at the Thurstons, one by one. It may as well have been a sword, for with every thrust of her finger, they flinched as if impaled. "And you would've let me take the blame? How utterly despicable."

Miss Thurston blushed and fiddled with her gloves.

"Unforgivable, I vow."

"I should think so." Lady Ravensdale set Freddy aside and delivered the Thurstons a hair- singeing look.

Brette faced her sister and Raven. "Rest assured, I have learned my lesson well, and shall never again do anything more daring than wear blue stockings. Nonetheless, my heart's at peace because my intentions were pure."

She marched to the door, but before leaving, leveled each person present a stony look. "I made a mistake, and I own my part in this bumblebroth. But each of you was ready to convict me, when in fact, they," she swept her hand toward the unrepentant Thurstons, "should be reproved for their fiendish plot."

From Alex's position beside the window, the woundedness in Brette's lovely sea-green eyes stabbed him. They'd misjudged her, though the circumstances did make her look guilty as sin.

She angled her head regally, and the candles' reflected off the bright tresses. "Danfield is well rid of you, Ophelia."

Mrs. Thurston huffed, "Well, I never..." Ophelia's face crumpled, and she sniffled. *She* dared to cry?

"You might find him dull, but at least he's a man of character and not a lying, deceptive charlatan." Brette's angled jaw revealed her injured pride.

Tiny imp she might be, but her feistiness more than compensated for her lack of stature. As the smallest Culpepper, how challenging it must have been when the others towered above her, their height giving the impression of power and authority.

But the petite spitfire before them? Alex would lay a wager that in a battle of wits, she'd verbally slay them all. Including him.

"I am retiring to my room to pack, and tomorrow I'll be away to— I suppose that's for you to decide, Lord Ravensdale. No doubt a place far from Town." She met Alex's gaze for an instant. *Because she knows I share her view?* "Where, I'll likely perish from inactivity and boredom."

Such exaggerated cynicism shaded her words, he barely refrained from laughing. How well he understood her reluctance. Raven did too, for until he married Brooke, he'd abhorred the country. For a week or two, provincial life might be tolerated, but months on end? No, thank you. One cow looked much the same as the other, and the abundance of rodents and insects, not to mention the early hours...

Again. No. Thank. You.

"Good riddance, I say," Thurston snapped, yanking Alex to the present unpleasant situation. Freddy raised his graying muzzle and growled.

Exactly so.

"I'll remind you, Thurston," Raven intoned, his irritation tangible, "you're speaking of my ward, and had you, your wife, or your daughter possessed better characters, none of this would've happened."

Leventhorpe indicated the door with a sweep of his arm. "I'll thank you to leave my house and not return."

Muttering their indignation, the Thurstons filed past Brette.

She spared them no measure, meeting each of their sulky gazes with accusation and condemnation in hers.

"Please forgive me, Brette. I used your kindness woefully. That was unpardonable." Miss Thurston's apology earned her a tight, closed-mouth ribbon of a smile, but no more.

"If you'll excuse me, I must pack." Brette bobbed a shallow curtsy.

"Brette, darling, don't be hasty." Lady Ravensdale extended her hand. "There's no need to make an impulsive decision. Is there, Raven?"

Raven fairly melted beneath his wife's entreating eyes. He raked his hand through his hair. "Brette?"

Tucking her head to her chest, Brette glided from the room. No music filtered into the study this time. Had Lady Leventhorpe sent her guests to bed early?

Tears had glistened in Brette's eyes as she left. Alex

would swear to it, and the desire to protect her seared him, hot and fierce. He'd like to plant Thurston a facer. Might make his protruding nose look better afterward, but rectors didn't keep their positions if they popped men's corks, no matter how justified.

Lady Ravensdale made to follow her sister.

"Let her go, my dear." Raven tucked his wife's hand into the crook of his arm. "She's humiliated and frustrated. Give her until tomorrow to calm and collect herself."

Brette would need more than a night to accomplish that.

Alex plucked a piece of lint from his arm. "My parish sponsors a foundling home, and I am seeking additional patronage for a ragged school I wish to start. Both are in need of directors, as well as volunteers."

He summoned his most beguiling smile. The one that sickened him and made him feel like a fawning toady. Or a coquette after a new gewgaw from her protector. Another thing he loathed about his position: the groveling to gain support for charities.

He'd little pride left, but what he did stung sharply.

Not that he didn't think the causes worthwhile. He did, of course.

If he possessed the means, he would've established a school for the performing arts too. Though when he'd shared the notion at White's a couple of years ago, the incredulous chortles rang in his ears for months afterward.

Ironic. The Season couldn't officially start until the Royal Academy of Art's annual Exhibition, but should a fellow suggest a school for actors, vocalists, dancers, and musicians...

Ah, well. Nothing but a fanciful dream.

On the whole, the rich didn't like parting with their coin unless it benefited them, and performers, no matter their degree of talent or pedigree, were relegated to Society's lowest ranks. "Perhaps an arrangement can be made, and Miss Culpepper can put her skills to use helping others, rather than being banished to the countryside."

"Oh, yes. That's a marvelous idea." Lady Ravensdale seized the notion like a drowning sailor tossed a flotation. "Please say you'll consider it, Heath. Brette's not like the rest of us. She'd waste away in the provinces. She hasn't voiced it, but she much prefers the city. I've never seen her as animated and happy as when we came to Town."

"I suppose, Hawk, you'd like Leventhorpe and me to fund this school of yours? And make a generous donation to the foundling home as well?" Raven's wry smile told Alex all he needed to know.

He'd get his school. Eventually. More vitally, Brette would be spared temporary exile.

"If you feel convicted to do so." Alex bowed his head.

Another religious ploy. Use guilt, and spread it thickly. He'd become quite adept at the practice but loathed himself as a consequence. He longed to be his true self once more. Not a puppet directed by obligation and expectation.

He scratched his eyebrow, suddenly weary to his bones. "I must return to London Monday next, in any event. If it's convenient, Miss Culpepper and her abigail may travel with me. I do have to stop in at High Wycombe on the way, however. I promised my sisters and cousin I would the next time I traveled nearby."

He'd made that promise three visits to the countryside ago, and his conscience chafed him for his reluctance.

Truthfully, he'd rather not call at High Wycombe at all. The youngest of four, Alex had been the only son and a sickly child, as well as his mother's favorite. His sisters still called him Little Alex, Mother's pet name for him. They and his second cousin, Arthur, the Earl of Wycombe, had pestered him for two years now to find a wife. He couldn't fathom why they deemed his marrying any of their business.

Wycombe had his heir, Lawrence. Alex needn't produce one also. And their scolding and nagging wasn't because they'd found marital bliss. Alex gave a soft snort. No, indeed.

Of his sisters' unions, two had been arranged matches, the other a marriage of convenience.

Wycombe had surrendered to the parson's mousetrap for money; a gross amount, truth to tell. Each seemed as content as one might, given their situations. None of them had ever aspired to marry for affection and viewed leg-shackling as beneficial business arrangement.

Rather cold-hearted and mercenary.

Alex might have relinquished his former life, conceded to family expectations, and become a reverend—after all, what other prospects did he have? Living off his friends' charity indefinitely?—but hounds' teeth, he wouldn't settle when he selected a wife.

Not true. He'd settle, because she wouldn't be Brette.

Picturing her as a cleric's wife, he choked on a suppressed laugh. Lord, wouldn't that be something?

Might alleviate the tediousness of his profession, but she'd be miserable. He'd nothing to offer her anyway, except a charming smile and ready laugh.

Chambers cleared his throat. Why hadn't he promptly left after Miss Thurston's abrupt arrival? As trained to do, he'd disappeared into the room's shadows, temporarily forgotten until he might interrupt.

Leventhorpe pressed two fingers to his forehead, tension tightening his face. This house party wouldn't soon be forgotten, and he despised being gossip fodder. "Was there something else, Chambers?"

Chambers stepped forward and extended a missive to Raven. "Yes, sir. Please forgive the informality and lack of salver, but the messenger claims the matter is most urgent. You're to read it at once, my lord. He's ridden straight from London and awaits your reply below stairs."

Raven accepted the dirty, crumpled letter. A slight frown veed his brows as he inspected the folded paper. "It's from a solicitor. A Mr. Horace Shipwreck, and it's also addressed to Brette."

Lady Ravensdale arched a fine blond brow. "Really? How peculiar. I'm positive we aren't acquainted with him."

"Never heard of him either," Alex agreed.

Raven broke the seal with his thumb and quickly perused the contents. His flexing jaw and whoosh of suddenly released breath didn't bode well.

"What is it?" Lady Ravensdale laid her hand on his

arm, and Freddy sat up, head cocked and ears twitching. "Bad news?"

"Shall I give the messenger a reply?" Chambers asked, his features an indecipherable mask.

His composure hadn't cracked the tiniest amount this entire party.

Raven glanced at Brooke then shook his head. "Not presently, Chambers. See that he's fed." He faced Leventhorpe. "Trist, can I impose upon you to allow the chap to sleep in the servant's quarters tonight?"

"Of course." Leventhorpe nodded, though curiosity and concern glimmered in his eyes. "Chambers, please oversee the arrangements. Oh, and send a rider after Drake and Whitehouse, unless they've returned already."

"At once, my lord." The servant closed the door behind him, and Alex took it upon himself to pour a finger's worth of brandy for all present.

Intuition or perhaps a holy prompting told him they'd need the bracing spirit.

After the butler left, Raven lifted the paper. "What I'm about to reveal stays in our inner circle. It's imperative this information is kept confidential."

Alex handed Raven and Lady Ravensdale their tumblers.

"Thank you, no." Her ladyship set hers aside.

Blast. Alex had forgotten that she was increasing.

"I'll take hers." Raven quaffed his before gulping hers too. Something had him thoroughly disjointed. A rare occurrence.

Alex took a measured sip. "May I presume the contents aren't welcome news?"

The taut lines outlining Raven's mouth answered before he did. "No."

"Well, are you going to tell us, or do we have to play charades to find out?" Leventhorpe tossed back his brandy then banged his tumbler onto his desk, causing Brooke to start. He grinned sheepishly. "Sorry 'bout that."

Generally, Raven wasn't shy on words. Whatever the letter's contents, they'd flustered him. "Raven?" Alex calmly coached. "We're waiting."

Raven blew out a heavy breath and waved the dingy paper. It rattled in protest at his rude treatment. "This notifies us Brette's father has died, and she's inherited a decent sum."

Lady Ravensdale's eyebrows leaped in surprise, and she swiped a tendril from her forehead. "Father died more than five years ago, and I assure you, there were no funds left. This must be a perverse joke, or Mr. Shipwreck has the wrong person."

"No, I believe he has the correct person, my dear."

"He can't possibly," she objected. "It makes no sense."

"According to this letter," frowning at the creased rectangle, Raven took his wife's hand, "Brette isn't your sister, after all, but rather another cousin..."

Every bit of color drained from Lady Ravensdale's face.

"...and her father was," he rubbed his thumb atop the back of her hand in a comforting gesture, "an actor of some renown."

4

Early the next morning, her trunks neatly packed and stacked beside her bedchamber door, Brette marched downstairs. Straightening the lace cuff of one of her favorite traveling gowns, a simple jonquil and ivory ensemble, she quirked her mouth. She'd taken extra pains with her appearance this morning. Who couldn't use a mite extra confidence in a situation like hers?

Resolution stiffened her spine.

Silly, punishing her when the Thurstons had manipulated the entire situation.

She'd meant what she'd promised about foregoing her matchmaking jaunts, however. No more. Two disasters were plenty.

Now how would she occupy her time? Embroider a

ship's cargo hold of unmentionables?

With luck, Heath would send her to Culpepper Park. At least she knew people in the area and could anticipate a few invitations until her banishment ended.

This morning, she fancied a hearty breakfast before she trundled off to wherever Heath decided she ought to go. As she approached the dining room, laughter filtered from the open doors, and her steps faltered. She hadn't expected anyone to be about yet. Or at least not that many people. The room fairly buzzed with chatter, rustling paper, clinking and clanking china, and an occasional laugh.

At the threshold, she mustered a smile for—

Good heavens. Truly?

Brooke, Brette's three cousins, Heath, Alex, Lieutenant Drake, Captain Whitehouse, and Lord Leventhorpe sat at the table, chatting amiably.

The entire family, as well as the rogues, awake and dressed at half past seven? Most unusual. An eyebrow crept high onto her forehead. And highly— *exceedingly*—suspicious. She supposed she ought to be grateful that the other guests had more sense than to rise so early, else they'd witness her chastisement too.

Nothing for it. She put on a cheerful countenance and entered.

"Happy morning to you. I'm surprised everyone's

awake this early." She slid onto the chair the butler held for her. "Thank you, Chambers."

"Tea or hot chocolate, Miss Culpepper?" He held a gold-edged, sapphire blue cup in his white-gloved hand. Did he give her a slight wink?

"Tea, please." Brette arranged her serviette on her lap and raised her head. "I take it you've risen early to give me a grand send off? Most considerate. Where am I away to?"

Please let it be Culpepper Park and not Heath's estate.

She had the distinct impression the staff at Walcotshire Park, though pleasant enough, found the Culpeppers short of the mark.

Chambers placed her teacup and a full plate before her; ham and waffles, her favorite breakfast. A rare treat indeed. His doing, no doubt, the dear.

"Do you require anything else, miss?"

Though his formal demeanor didn't give the slightest hint, he was a soft old bear beneath his perfect suit. She'd taken to sharing tea with him and Cook on the days she ventured into the kitchen to bake one treat or other. No one at Bristledale court knew she made half the biscuits, tartlets, and other sweetmeats they nibbled daily.

She fancied owning her own chocolate shop and

serving dainties and other delicacies. But gently-born women didn't labor for their living. She might have if Brooke and Blythe hadn't married well, but now that she boasted an earl for a brother-in-law and a marquis for a cousin, a quaint storefront was out of the question.

Ridiculous social rules.

"This is perfect. Thank you." What better way to be bundled off in disgrace then after indulging in her favorite breakfast?

"Chambers? We require a few moments' privacy."

Lord Leventhorpe's casual request didn't fool Brette, though taking her to task with an audience seemed a speck beyond necessary.

Besides, it wasn't his place, unless he'd decided, as Bristledale's lord, that he should have his say as well. Beyond the pale, nevertheless, for the captain and lieutenant to be privy to her humiliation. After all, they weren't family.

At least not yet.

Given the gentlemen's attentiveness to the twins, she suspected they strove to remedy that situation.

She would not help them.

No, she absolutely would not.

After Chambers ushered the footmen from the dining room, he carefully closed the door. He probably stood guard outside, giving a gimlet eye to anyone who dared venture near.

Taking a sip of tea, she braced herself for the worst.

Maybe they'd decided to send her elsewhere besides the countryside. Like the university in Switzerland Blaire and Blaike were off to in a few weeks. *God help me*. No desire, whatsoever, nudged Brette to traipse across the continent and freeze her backside off in the Swiss Alps. The cold caused her nose to turn rosy and drip most embarrassingly.

She far preferred dancing at Almack's or another assembly room. Not that she minded further instruction. Just not thousands of miles from England. In fact, if she'd owned the resources, she'd start a woman's college in here. Absurd that only men were permitted the privilege of continuing their education.

She dared study Alex from beneath her lashes and caught her breath when she found him regarding her from beneath his lowered lids. A wry smile tugged his handsome mouth upward at the corners, and she couldn't help but smile in return when he gave her a conspiratorial wink.

Quite the pair they were. Neither fit where they'd been thrust, though each did their best to make their circumstances work. A sense of humor and a positive attitude helped.

Raven put down his fork and knife, the clanking

drawing her attention to him and Brooke.

Her sister's encouraging smile sent a jot of hope through Brette. Perhaps she wasn't to be cloistered after all.

Patting her mouth with her serviette, she surveyed those assembled. Why rally the troops then? A mite much, particularly since she barely knew the captain or lieutenant. Well, the sooner she heard what her sentence was, the sooner she could accept her fate and be on her way.

"I presume you want to tell me what you've decided. I'll admit I'm astonished you choose to do so while breaking our fast, Heath." She speared a small piece of ham.

Blaire grinned as she raised her chocolate cup. "No more surprised than we were when Brooke dragged Blaike and me from bed before the sun rose."

"I don't remember the last time I awoke this early." Blaike hid a dainty yawn behind her hand. "But the sunrise was spectacular."

"You should view it from a ship's deck." Captain Whitehouse's grin creased his tanned face. "Truly magnificent."

"Well, I suppose I shall when Blaire and I are off to school." Her cheeks pinkening, she took a dainty bite of toast. Her features sobered as she chewed, and she set the toast on her plate. "I heard your latest matchmaking antics went slightly awry, Brette."

"My dear cousin, slightly doesn't begin to describe the disaster. But the calamity ended much better than it might have." Nonetheless, Brette was quite done with ventures of that nature. "Now I must face the consequences, which, I presume, is why you're all here."

A slightly guarded expression on his features, Alex relaxed into his chair, one hand resting on the tablecloth. Now and again, he drummed his fingertips—the right forefinger ink-stained— as if troubled.

Brette scrutinized those seated again. Call it intuition, instinct, or fey, but her skin prickled ominously as something leaden and gloppy, like congealed day old porridge, settled in her stomach. Something else was wrong besides last night's escapade. She put her fork down, her appetite having flown.

"What's going on?"

Heath stood and straightened his already tidy coat. "I've changed my mind. I think it best to have this conversation in private."

"As I advised you." Alex sent Raven a stern look before his gaze drifted to Brette.

Compassion simmered there.

Botheration. Was her fate truly so bad he felt compelled to protect her?

"Why tell me in seclusion? I'm sure everyone is already aware. I promise you, I shan't dissolve into tears." She might later, but never, ever in public.

Brooke leaned forward and clasped Brette's hand. "Brette, dearest. It seems..." She paused but, after drawing a ragged breath, plowed onward. "A letter from a solicitor arrived last night. He claims you're the daughter of an actor named Reginald Wiley."

"Pardon?" Her mouth gone dry as desert sand, Brette swallowed then licked her lips. "Pardon?" she squeaked again, despite her constricting throat.

I sound like a blasted parrot.

Her sleepless night must've had her hearing things. "That's impossible. We've the same parents, Brooke."

Brooke nodded, the ringlets framing her face bouncing with the gesture. "Yes, I believed so too, but the letter mentions a Belinda. It states she was your mother and died giving birth to you."

"Do you believe that's true?" Brette laced her fingers together, squeezing them to maintain her composure. She darted everyone a brief glance before meeting Brooke's eyes once more.

After casting Heath a desperate look, Brooke bit her lower lip and gave a single affirmative nod. "I heard

Mama mention someone named Belinda to Papa one time. I was young, not more than five or six, I think. When I entered the room, Mama swiftly changed the subject. But not before she referred to Belinda as her sister."

"Dear God. Are you saying you're not my sister?"

The vice squeezing Brette's chest—merciless in its fierceness and intensity—hampered her breathing. Being trundled off to the country was a horrid enough fate, but this?

The daughter of an actor, not a gentleman farmer. Utterly scandalous by *le beau monde* standards.

If true, it explained the age difference between her and Brooke and why Brette's build was different than her cousins'. Judging by her petite frame, her father must have been a shrimpy thing.

All cousins. No sister.

"Oh, Brette, it doesn't make any difference." Blaike rushed to kneel beside Brette's chair.

She clasped Brette's hand, her lovely sapphire eyes pooling, though she bravely tried to blink the tears away. "We're still cousins, dear one."

In an instant, Blaire, too, kneeled beside Brette's chair. "We've been like sisters. I scarcely remember our parents. What I do remember is how the five of us," she took in each of the girls in turn, "always had each other."

"And that won't ever, ever change." Blythe shook her head vehemently as a single tear leaked from her eye and trickled down her cheek.

Leventhorpe rose to stand behind her chair, placing a comforting hand on his wife's shoulder, his adoration clear.

The men, rather than looking uncomfortable and awkward, gazed at Brette with sincere sympathy and kindness, and she trapped her lower lip to stifle a sob. She did not cry in public. But the compassion, surely that was all it was, radiating from Alex nearly caused her to lose her tenuous grip on her control.

If she hadn't known otherwise, she would've thought he ached for her. Felt her pain.

"Why would our parents—your parents—keep something so significant from us?" Brette could barely get the words out. A peculiar ringing in her ears, combined with the inability to draw a decent breath and the grayish-black flecks dancing before her eyes, had her truly concerned she might swoon—face-first, into her waffle.

You do not swoon, faint, or have fits of the vapors, Brette Anastasia Wiliminia Culpepper.

Stop wallowing in self-pity this instant.

The room fell silent and everyone except Brette exchanged concerned or hesitant glances.

Don't tell me there's more? How could there possibly be more awfulness?

Heath cleared his throat. "We don't know for certain, Brette, and that's why we'll journey to London straightaway to speak with the solicitor who sent the missive."

"But?" Brette dug her nails into her palms. Given the consternation on his face, she wasn't going to like what he had to say.

"Brette, darling." Brooke clasped Brette's hand atop the lace tablecloth. "Mr. Shipwreck gave no indication your parents ever married."

A bastard?

Heath patted Brooke's shoulder as she dissolved into tears.

"Holy Chr—" Lieutenant Drake swore, but cut the vulgarity short at Heath's severe glare.

Captain Whitehouse released a low whistle and shook his head, his long hair brushing his collar.

So, Drake and Whitehouse hadn't been aware after all.

Heath and Leventhorpe, Alex too, must have placed a great deal of trust in the pair to make them privy to this damaging information. God help her if they possessed loose tongues or a penchant for *on dit*. They didn't seem the sort, but...

Hauling her focus upward, Brette met Alex's troubled jade eyes over the dahlia and lily centerpiece. Steam rose in lazy, silvery tendrils from his ignored cup of tea. Did the same torment reflect in her eyes that shone in his? He appeared utterly devastated, in a composed, manly sort of way.

Interesting how much a person's eyes revealed.

A hysterical laugh bubbled up the back of her throat, and Brette flexed her jaw and balled her hands to subdue it.

That rattlepate Miss Thurston's self-caused ruination paled in comparison to this.

When word of Brette's low birth leaked out, she'd be shunned. Shamed. Refused admittance to homes she'd cordially been invited into before. Unless she married a wealthy, titled peer, she'd never set foot in polite society again. She'd be an albatross around her family's necks. The embarrassing relation to be avoided, sent away, lest she bring disgrace on them too.

From where she mustered the strength to stand, she didn't know. "If you'll excuse me, please. I find I need a few moments to myself."

The rest of the men stood, somber-faced all.

"We'll depart as soon as we're packed, Brette." Heath came round to her side of the table, and like an older, caring brother, wrapped her in his embrace. "You needn't fear. We can keep this secret contained."

About as contained as a spark in a haystack.

Soon, the ember would ignite a blaze no amount of water could extinguish. Word would get out. No force on earth could prevent it.

Mayhap Alex's prayers were her only chance for deliverance.

"Everyone in this room would die to protect you." Heath leaned back and his lips bent before he angled his head, indicating the entrance. "And a concerned butler, too."

The French windows clearly outlined Chambers's distinct profile. He didn't worry her. He'd bite off his tongue before saying a word against her. However, the round-eyed maid turning tail and rushing for the servants' entrance, her apron strings flapping in her haste, couldn't be trusted.

Brette allowed herself a bitter smile as Heath followed her gaze and swore.

"Fiend seize it."

"Within the hour, everyone at Bristledale Court will know of my circumstances, and it won't take a week for word to reach London." She did laugh, a sad, haunting rasp. "Don't you think it rather ironic, that I, who fancied myself a matchmaker, am illegitimate and won't ever marry now?"

"Don't say that, Brette." Brooke rushed to her side and cupped her cheek. "There are plenty of men who'd be honored to call you wife."

Brette blinked against scorching tears. "Name one."

Alex met her gaze square on, a gentle smile teasing his firm mouth. "I would."

A wise woman knows life and
love do not obey our expectations but they do
obey our intentions, though in ways never anticipated.
~Appearances and Attitude—The Genteel Lady's
Guide to Practical Living

5

Alex drummed his fingertips on the plush crimson seat he sat upon.

More of Leventhorpe's generosity.

Alex's gig was fine for tooling around London, but he relied upon his friends' benevolence for lengthier trips. He'd depended on them for a whole lot more over the years. One reason why, without other prospects, he'd grudgingly filled his maternal uncle's position as St. Peter's rector. If he hadn't assumed the role, for the first time in over one hundred years, no member of his mother's family would head the parish; as he'd been admonished repeatedly by his manipulative, perhaps even well-intended, family. Guilt proved a powerful motivator.

With each jolt of the equipage, Alex's insides

cramped a fraction more.

He anticipated visits to High Wycombe with the same enthusiasm as being bled or leeched. Childhood memories of the ghastly procedures made him wince and his stomach knot. Damned lucky he'd lived to adulthood with all the quackery practiced on him because of Mother's constant fretting.

He'd intentionally timed this trip to avoid Wycombe. The glorious twelfth of August found his cousin gadding to his hunting lodge for a few weeks of grouse hunting. According to family gossip, he spent more time stalking and fishing than attending to his earldom, likely the reason behind Alex's summons to High Wycombe.

Alex hadn't committed to a particular day, rather having promised he'd visit in the late summer or early autumn, when his parish could more readily spare him. With an assistant curate eager to prove his capabilities, Alex needn't fear St. Peter's would suffer from his absences.

He may have also neglected to tell the curate where he'd be. Another deliberate oversight, and one which had prompted the bishop to write him on more than one occasion, suggesting Alex devote more time to his parish and less to his pre-ministry cohorts. And yet here he was, dutifully, if somewhat tardily, attending to his familial summons while disregarding his clerical responsibilities.

And for what?

Other than spending an enjoyable day or two with his numerous nieces and nephews, his trips to High Wycombe usually proved a colossal waste of time. Robust and arrogantly confident, Wycombe ignored Alex's suggestions. Consequently, he'd stopped offering advice years ago. He'd agreed to this visit to pacify his sisters and Mary, the Countess of Wycombe, who fussed about her son's future.

At the rate Wycombe blew through blunt, Lawrence might inherit an impoverished estate, which, no doubt, infuriated the countess. She'd brought a fortune to the union, but once she'd murmured, "I do," she'd retained no control beyond a quid or two. The earl's neglect of the estate and tenants had taken a harsh toll, and the countess had confided in Alex's sisters that she feared they neared financial ruin.

How could Wycombe possibly have exhausted his fortune—his wife's fortune—so swiftly?

Had he mortgaged the estate too?

Then again, when he stabled nearly one hundred horses and half as many hunting hounds, not to mention his obsession with whores, guns, and brandy, it shouldn't have come as a surprise.

The trees parted overhead, allowing Alex a peek of bright, cloudless sky. In the meadow visible through the trunks, he glimpsed a red stag, head raised nobly, horns gleaming underneath the late afternoon sun. A lake, surrounded on three sides by towering pines, glistened blue-green.

The same color as Brette's eyes.

He closed his to block the astonished expressions on everyone's faces at breakfast this morning—her utter incredulity the absolute worst. She hadn't believed his marriage offer—had in fact thought he jested or felt sorry for her. He'd never be so cruel or insensitive. He'd been desperate to smooth the devastation ravaging her lovely face, and the words had spilled from his mouth without conscious thought. Nevertheless, though impromptu, he'd meant them.

He loved her.

Ever since she'd grinned and cheekily suggested he was a valet, his stupid heart willingly lay prostrate at her feet. Of course, having just met her, he couldn't declare himself, and now she believed he but pitied her.

At his declaration this morning, she'd laughed, a husky, watery combination of pain and skepticism.

"Oh, Alex, I wouldn't ever let you make such a sacrifice. Can you imagine what the Church would say? How your parish would react to you marrying a by-blow?" She'd shaken her glossy blond head, her pearl earrings bobbing. "I do thank you for your kind offer. It means more than you can know."

His first proposal, perhaps his only, politely turned down.

To their credit, not one of his friends, not even Leventhorpe, famous for his sarcasm and biting wit, had ribbed Alex about his pronouncement. They knew him too bloody well. Knew he'd been serious.

Their pity galled.

He didn't care in the least whether Brette was legitimate. He did care about *her*, however, and she'd been delivered a devastating blow. She knew the censure she'd endure when the *ton* learned of her birth.

If Raven were wise, he'd quickly find her a husband and send them on an extended wedding trip.

Alex's gut quivered, and he smirked. It wouldn't be him.

Her rejection didn't come as a surprise. She had no interest in a cleric's wife's dull, placid life. She'd probably shock the parishioners with something outrageous. Say, waltzing on Sundays. What a wonderful life. Dancing with her after services until they became too aged and decrepit to stand upright.

As he whistled a favorite, soothing hymn, the carriage turned onto High Wycombe's meandering drive. How many times had he taken this same journey, never with any real enthusiasm?

Majestic oaks, more than a century old, lined the half-mile path. Their dying leaves, in glorious hues ranging from scarlet to apricot, fluttered high above. A brownish-gray hare hopped beneath a bush and raised onto its hind legs, nose twitching and paws poised as it stared at the rumbling giant passing by.

Alex closed his eyes and spoke a very real prayer. God help him get through the next two days, especially if Grandmama was in residence.

His sisters fussed and fretted over him almost as badly as his mother had. And he could expect extra rich delicacies and likely tonics and tinctures sneaked into his food. Last visit, they'd given him a purging concoction, and he'd sprinted to the necessary every half an hour the first day.

By Jove, this time, he'd put his foot down.

He wasn't a sickly lad, and they needed to stop treating him like he'd cock up his toes if he sneezed. At least Wycombe treated him like a man, in his condescending, superior, everyone-is-beneath-me sort of way.

Alex could already hear Grandmama clamoring on about his duty to the earldom. *Just in case, God forbid,* something happened to Wycombe. She'd probably compiled a list of misses she considered eligible, too. No doubt empty-headed chits the difficult old tabby considered malleable.

No wonder the current countess had banished the dowager to her dower house and rarely permitted her to set foot within the manor. Maybe he'd be spared and Grandmama wouldn't be in residence. A small, but most welcome reprieve, if that were the case.

Alex would've been hard-pressed to determine whether class snobbery more afflicted Wycombe, his countess, or Grandmama. In Wycombe's case, the superiority was sadly misplaced.

Time had treated Alex far kinder than his cousin. A decade his senior, bald, round as an apple, and given to indigestion, Wycombe had aged much faster. A life of dissipation and idleness did that to a fellow.

A bird's trill echoed from the treetops, and Alex mimicked it. Lowering the window, he began whistling. Often confined to bed as a boy, he'd taught himself the skill and had learned to imitate several birds quite well.

The coach drew to a stop before his ancestors' stately home, more castle than manor. Tall turrets graced the northern and southern corners, and Roman god statues topped the stone pillars on either side of the grand stairs leading to an imposing entrance. Row upon row of mullioned windows, many set with glorious colored glass images, covered the house's front.

After descending from the coach, he permitted himself a rather uncouth yawn and stretched his arms wide. Two Dalmatians loped to his side, their tails wagging in welcome. "Hallo, boys. Jasper, you've gotten fatter than the last time I saw you." He rubbed behind the dog's ears. "And Clyde, you're sporting more silver on your muzzle. Very distinguished, I must say."

Clyde also received a few pets upon his head.

A moment later, another Dalmatian, smaller and finer-boned, cautiously approached. Five pudgy, clumsy puppies trailed her. Smitten at once, Alex crouched low and cooed softly. "Come here. It's all right. I shan't hurt you." He cocked a brow at the two males. "And which of you chaps is the father of this fine family?"

Jasper bumped the female's nose before sniffing the pups' wee rumps. Clyde plopped his rear on the drive and proceeded to cleanse himself with a great deal of loud slurping and snuffling.

Well, that answered that question.

One bold pup waddled over to Alex and cautiously smelled his boot. Alex wiggled his toes, and, growling, the puppy pounced on his foot. Alex laughed and lifted the sturdy fellow. "Hello there. Aren't you a fine lad?"

The pup licked his face, and Alex chuckled again. He kissed the dog's nose. "I wonder if I can persuade the countess to part with you. Would you like that?"

The pup answered by biting Alex's ear. "Ouch, you tiny terror. That hurt."

"Sir, I am pleased you have finally arrived."

Holding the pup to his shoulder, Alex pivoted.

Stokes, the butler, stood at the entrance, his expression drawn, though not critical. He'd aged since Alex last visited.

"Her ladyship will receive you in the ivory drawing room. She's been awaiting your arrival for days."

She had?

As Alex placed the pup on the ground, guilt kicked her knobby toes into his ribs.

His deliberate vagueness as to his arrival reflected poorly on him. Already prone to nervousness, poor Lady Wycombe had likely demanded her footmen keep a constant vigil for him. A beautiful woman, vain in the extreme, the countess wasn't one typically caught unawares. She took great pains with her appearance and never, *ever* breached decorum.

In short, few met her impossible standards.

After plucking several stiff dog hairs from his jacket, Alex ran up the steps. "It's nice to see you too, Stokes."

Stokes took Alex's measure from toe to top, lingering on the white hairs stubbornly attached to his functional black coat. The countess would not be pleased.

"Looks like I rolled in a kennel." Alex chuckled, brushing at his jacket. "How fare you?" One didn't generally inquire of the servants, but as a cleric, he felt obliged to ask, and

Stokes... Poor chap, it appeared he'd been trampled by the hounds cavorting in the drive.

"As well as can be expected under the circumstances, sir." He bowed his silvery head and indicated Alex should precede him. "If you please."

Alex drew his brows together. "Stokes, is everything all right? You seem ... troubled." Stokes stopped abruptly, and Alex plowed into him on the threshold. "Beg your pardon."

Thoroughly nonplussed for an instant, the normally imperturbable butler drew in a bracing breath and squared his shoulders. "May I presume you did not receive the correspondence her ladyship sent?"

Did disapproval color his voice?

Alex offered an apologetic smile, hoping to breach the stuffy old boy's defenses. "I'm afraid not. I've been away from London for nearly three weeks."

Stokes's nose inched upward. "I see."

See what?

Alex stepped onto the glossy parquet floor. As they had for his entire life, his grandparents' serious countenances stared at him from their ornately framed portraits above the double arched stairways. "Is there something I ought to know before I meet with the countess?"

"Stokes? Is that Alexander?" Lady Wycombe's refined, yet slightly cold voice inquired from a room farther along the corridor. "Do stop dawdling and show him in."

Rather than tactlessly shout down the passageway in response, Stokes instead calmly extended his hand. "Your hat and gloves, sir?"

After Stokes laid them on the marble-topped table, he again gestured for Alex to precede him. "I believe it best for the countess to apprise you."

Such secretiveness.

Likely, Wycombe had finally exhausted her wealth or fathered another by-blow. At last count, he boasted three daughters by three different mistresses. Lady Wycombe had provided him his heir, thirteen year-old Lawrence, and except for his mother's auburn hair, he was an exact replica of his papa, right down to his chubby, red cheeks.

Alex strode into the drawing room, and the countess gracefully rose, pale as milk in an ebony gown. Odd her rising, and odder still her choice of gown. Probably a new trend he wasn't aware of. Always dressed in the first stare of fashion, she enjoyed playing queen of the parlor, and usually when gentlemen called, lifted her hand to be fawned over.

He bent into a courtier's gallant bow.

She liked groveling too and remained obtuse to his

mockery.

A wonder The Almighty hadn't smote him long before this for his sins. Was there ever a less rector-like man to declare himself God's servant? Actually, yes. Lancelot Blackburn, a notorious pirate, became an archbishop, proving redemption and transformation were possible even for the worst of wretches. So why didn't that tidbit ease Alex's self-castigation?

"Really, Alexander. I anticipated you days and days ago. It's been ever so difficult, and you were needed. I've already sent a footman to your sisters with word of your belated arrival. They're expected here shortly."

She drew a filmy handkerchief sort of thing from her sleeve and dabbed her eyes, mindful not to smudge her carefully applied cosmetics. Truly a stunning creature, but frigid as the River Thames in winter.

She sniffled, and he squinted.

Were those *real* tears?

He hadn't believed her capable. And why had the troublesome trio been summoned?

He'd intended to call briefly, *very briefly*, at each of his three sisters' houses before continuing to London tomorrow. Though his curator was an excellent cleric, better than Alex could ever hope to be, Alex couldn't remain absent any longer. The bishop only claimed so much patience. Truly, Dalton deserved the position more than Alex did. He enjoyed the work, loved the parish and her people.

He'd actually chosen the profession. Imagine that.

Alex offered Lady Wycombe his brightest clergyman's smile. The one declaring, *Fear not, I'm at your disposal and shall make everything right.* "Tell me what troubles you. Perhaps I can help."

She froze, handkerchief at her ever so lightly rouged cheek and her China doll eyes widened. "Did you not receive my letter?" She huffed indignantly. "I posted it three weeks ago."

"I've been attending various house parties, most recently as a guest of the Marquis of Leventhorpe." Must she be so miffed? He wasn't accountable to her. "No doubt the letter's stacked neatly atop my desk, awaiting my arrival home."

The countess flopped—actually flopped so firmly her perfect cylinder curls pirouetted—onto the settee upholstered in fuchsia brocade and trimmed in cream braid. She wadded her handkerchief into a ball, unwadded it then wrung the tortured cloth between her hands.

"Oh, dear me, dear me."

"I take it something's amiss?" Alex slowly sank into a chair opposite her.

Typically, she never showed her agitation, but rather kept her emotions hidden behind icy disdain.

"Amiss? I should say so. Wycombe and

Lawrence..." Clamping her eyes shut, she drew in a shuddery breath, her lower lip quivering. Her lids crept upward, and such anguish glimmered in the moist depths that Alex sucked in a swift gulp of air.

"What has happened? Have they taken ill? Been injured?" He racked his brain. Who was the best physician in London? "I'm acquainted with several excellent doctors—"

"It's much too late for that, Alexander." She swallowed, touching the wrinkled cloth to the corner of her eye once more. "Charlbury burned nearly to the ground." Anguish shook her wispy voice. "Only a footman and a maid escaped."

"Oh, my God, Mary."

Her sorrowful gaze wandered to her son's portrait above the fireplace's elaborate mahogany mantel.

"You are the Earl of Wycombe now."

Even the greatest of intentions become tragic
actions when delivered without careful thought.
*~Appearances and Attitude—The Genteel Lady's
Guide to Practical Living*

6

*Two Months Later
St. Peter's Foundling Home, London*

Brette laid the drowsy toddler beside another child already fast asleep on the thin pallet. After brushing a lock of hair from the girl's face, she straightened and searched the sterile room.

Alex's … Lord Wycombe's former parishioners either rocked infants or sorted clothing and other donations. Six-and-twenty children—the eldest not yet four years of age and the youngest barely two weeks—called this stark space home. And these counted as the fortunate ones. Older ragamuffins either lived on the streets, in orphanages, or in workhouses, the conditions beyond deplorable.

Three more sleeping quarters—equally as full as

this one—a kitchen, a director's office, a laundry, and a shabbily furnished sitting room completed the facility.

Silly to have hoped Alex might put in an appearance these past eight weeks she'd volunteered at St. Peter's. He wasn't rector any longer, after all. *Of course*, that wasn't why the carriage dropped her here promptly at ten and collected her at one o'clock three afternoons a week.

Well, perhaps it might be *one* of the reasons. The main motive. The other being atonement for her last matchmaking jaunt, which, in the end, had worked out remarkably well for everyone except her. Ophelia had married her Mr. Waters, and last week, Lord Danfield's banns had been read. Seems he'd found himself a bluestocking as entranced with stuffy tombs, musty mummies, and pooh-eating bugs as he. Even Phillip Lapley had managed to snare himself an American heiress.

Brette sighed and brushed her fingers over her brow.

Since the morning Alex had blurted he would marry her, she'd heard nothing from him. *Nothing.* Surely he regretted his outburst more than ever now that he'd unexpectedly inherited the earldom.

His news had reached their ears within days, coinciding with her reduced circumstances traveling the social circles. He'd attained the Society's highest elevation as she'd been relegated to the *le bon ton*'s cellar.

Her worn, but comfortable half-boots clacking on the cold, cement floor as she made her way to the kitchen, Brette curved her mouth into a self-deprecating smile and scratched her neck.

Hopefully, she hadn't acquired a flea or two.

What in the world would Alex have done if she had accepted and afterward he'd come into his title? What a bumblebroth that would have been.

A by-blow countess.

Gossip fodder for a Season or two, at the very least.

True, many people were born on the wrong side of the blanket; London teemed with them, as a matter of fact. They filled the beds in this establishment, poor, wretched darlings. But few, *very few*, rose to lofty or respectable heights.

Alex had simply been acting his usual kind self, and a warm sensation enveloped her each time she contemplated the noble, gallant gesture. She refused to closely examine the peculiar flickering behind her heart. No good could come of it. Not now, in any event.

Alex may not have believed he was destined for the Church, but his innate decency, humility, and compassion made him well-suited for the occupation, despite his misgivings. He hadn't anticipated coming into a title either, but she was sure, he'd do well by it.

How could he not? He cared more for others than himself.

Marching along the narrow passageway, desperately in need of a fresh coat of paint, she puckered her mouth at the lone piece of artwork in the entire place. A rather poor depiction of *The Last Supper*, hanging askew from a bent wire.

She stopped and straightened the lopsided painting. Disrespectful not to. Could she have made a go as a parson's wife?

She'd never know now, but rather thought the answer must be no. She too much enjoyed London's whirlwind of festivities to settle into a sedate, poised lifestyle. Just as well circumstances had taken this unexpected turn before her foolish heart completely succumbed to the golden-haired, green-eyed rogue's charm.

Too late.

Untying her apron, she winked at a big, brown-eyed toddler sucking her thumb and twirling her chestnut hair between thumb and forefinger.

Brette put a finger to her lips and mouthed, "Shh. Go to sleep."

The child grinned around her thumb and promptly

clamped her eyes shut.

Adorable cherub.

Brette arched her back and drew in a long, calming breath. After discovering her parentage, an ongoing restlessness had plagued her. Though grateful to have something to occupy her time—she did truly enjoy working with the unfortunate waifs—the discontentment still churned. More like simmered beneath her outwardly composed demeanor, and she half-expected the dissatisfaction to abruptly rise, bubbling and frothing, before spilling over and creating a mess far more intolerable than a thwarted elopement.

She and Heath had yet another appointment with Mr. Shipwreck this afternoon; a weekly occurrence since he'd sent his first disturbing missive. In fact, Heath should be here shortly to collect her, but Brooke, expecting their first child and suffering from morning sickness, had pleaded her excuses and wouldn't accompany them.

Thank God, Heath had taken Brette and her cousins under his wing. Hard to imagine she'd thought him the worst sort of ogre when they'd first met. Yes, indeed, he'd come around nicely.

A half smile teasing the edges of her mouth, she shook her head and removed her white crocheted cap. Wouldn't do to arrive at the solicitor's looking like a servant, but neither had she any desire to contract the louse plaguing the newly arrived children, hence the maid-like head covering. Releasing a breathy sigh, she draped the apron across a bent hook then hung the cap there too.

Her edginess might have been due to the reductions in invitations she'd received in recent weeks, although there weren't too terribly many routs, dinners, and assemblies in October ever.

Whether the trickling off of invites could be attributed to the time of year or the steady spread of her questionable parentage, she couldn't have said. She didn't really want to know, truth to tell.

Naturally, her family wouldn't say if they suspected the latter.

Stumbling across *Fanny Hill: Memoirs of a Woman of Pleasure* in Raven's library—most assuredly he hadn't a notion his shelves contained the scandalous volume—had provided her with several rather erotic hours of entertainment in the evenings.

My, the *interesting* facts one could learn from a book. Positively wicked, but utterly fascinating, too.

Since she'd likely end up a stuffy old tabby, she might as well educate herself on the mysteries that occurred between men and women. Unless she threw her morals to the wind, she would never experience intimacy herself.

Or bear children.

That knowledge hurt. Horribly.

Grossly unfair how in a blink of an eye, her life had been tossed hoof over tail, through no fault of her own. No wonder Mama had guarded the secret so closely. She hadn't expected the truth to come out, which must've meant she'd believed Brette's father had died or wanted no part of her life. Or—Brette feared this might be the real crux of the matter—Mama dreaded the scandal associated with raising a bastard niece.

Honestly, after learning of her pedigree, Brette had expected Raven to promptly remove the family, or at least her, to Walcotshire Park. He'd surprised her by insisting they remain in London, even after Blaire and Blaike, along with their lady's maids and a hired chaperone, sailed to the continent on Captain Whitehouse's ship. Lieutenant Drake had gallantly volunteered to go along to protect them. Or so he'd professed. His interest in Blaike hadn't gone unnoticed by Brette. However, her matchmaking days were truly over.

She missed the twins something awful. They'd been so excited at the prospect of attending college in Switzerland. Brette didn't share their enthusiasm, for her ambitions were much simpler: a quaint establishment on Finsbury Square that would make an excellent chocolate and pastry shop. She would learn this afternoon how much money she'd inherited from Reginald Wiley and, possibly, whether Mr. Shipwreck had determined if her parents ever married.

After donning her bonnet and pelisse in the home's shabby entrance, Brette gathered her gloves and reticule.

"Ah, yer off, are ye?" Mrs. Tuttle, the housekeeper, huffed along the passage. "The bairns favor ye, they do." She winked, her plump face folding like a giant fan. "Ye need yer own bairns. A whole passel. Some women are meant for motherhood. Ye be one of them."

A tiny ached thrummed in Brette's throat.

Impossible now. Unless she scampered to the country or a village and found a simple man who didn't care a whit about propriety or pedigree. With a family to love, she might not shrivel like grapes left in the sun.

"Yes, I'm afraid I must leave early today. I've an appointment and expect Lord Ravensdale directly." After wrapping her reticule's corded strap around her wrist, she slipped on a glove, taking care to modulate her voice. "Have you had word from Lord Wycombe?"

Breathing heavily, Mrs. Tuttle seized a chair and situated her ample girth atop it. She rubbed her chins and scrunched her eyes, deep in thought. "I think I did hear he'd sent a letter a day or two ago. Ye'd best ask Miss Yeatman. She be the one who opens and reads the post."

An hour later, Brette sliced Heath an astounded glance. She couldn't believe what she'd heard. "Are you saying I'm a wealthy woman, and I own two houses?"

Mr. Shipwreck squinted at her above his spectacles and inclined his head.

"Well, not Croesus or Midas rich, and I have no idea what the houses' conditions or worths are, but yes, you've received a respectable sum. Mr. Wiley invested wisely, and his will names you his sole survivor." He shuffled through a few papers, their brittle pages crackling and crunching. "It says here," he tapped a browned and raggedy-edged parchment, "your birth was chronicled at St. James, outside London."

Raven leaned forward. "Have you investigated her birth registration? Perhaps her parents' marriage was recorded there as well?"

How dear of him to continue to hope.

"It's possible. However, Wiley never mentioned marriage in his letters. Only his daughter, Miss—" He stopped fussing with the documents and, after pushing his spectacles up his nose for the twelfth or thirteenth time, gave her a kindly, closed-mouth smile. "I suppose I should ask what you prefer I call you."

"Please, call me Miss Culpepper. I cannot think of myself as anything else." How could she? "And to avoid further gossip, I think it's wisest."

"Very well. As I was saying, your father never mentioned marriage, just your mother's and aunt's names, your birth date, and where he registered your birth." He flipped over a few papers. "Ah, yes, and it seems he was the disowned and disgraced middle son of the Duke of Bellinghamshire." He glanced up. "Too bad, that. If I recall correctly, the estate passed to his grace's other surviving grandchild. A granddaughter, several years your junior, Miss Culpepper. Not the entailment, of course. But everything else."

Brette arched a brow and inclined her head. "Well, I suppose I should be suitably impressed."

She wasn't.

She would much prefer to continue as the daughter of Thomas and Bess Culpepper.

Raven gave her a teasing grin. "I am impressed. Granddaughter to old Fusty Boots himself. Well, well."

Brette chuckled, something she hadn't done much of lately. "Fusty Boots?"

"Let's say your grandfather wasn't a jovial sort, and his feet, er ... smelled." Heath's eyes twinkled.

"*Hmm.* Glad I don't take after him then. My mother ... Bess Culpepper knew of my father?" Bess would forever be the mother of her heart.

"That isn't clear." Mr. Shipwreck pointed at the file. "I have a letter from her stating she'd gladly take her sister's child and raise you as her own. She doesn't refer to your father." He sank into his chair's back and folded his hands across his abdomen. "If I may speak plainly?"

"By all means." Brette stopped twirling her reticule's silk tassel. All this dancing around politesse seemed a waste of time. What did Mr. Shipwreck fear she'd do? Become hysterical? Swoon? Break the absolutely hideous dog-dressed-as-sailor-in-a-tub inkwell atop his desk?

Honestly, destroying the ugly thing would be an act of mercy to one and all.

"In all probability, Miss Culpepper, your parents weren't married, and if they were, I'll wager the crown, they did so in secret. Even a disgraced duke's son doesn't marry an actress."

"I assumed as much." She couldn't prevent her disappointed sigh. She'd hoped differently, of course. For pity's sake, who wouldn't?

"Your father was a renowned rake and womanizer. From what I've been able to uncover, your mother ran off and became an actress. That's how they met. When she died giving birth, he couldn't be burdened with a child, let alone a newborn, and contacted me to locate Belinda's next of kin. He knew she was related to the Culpeppers."

Perfect. She'd been sired by a rapscallion, and he'd abandoned her.

Mr. Shipwreck scratched his rather prominent nose and gave her what he probably supposed was a reassuring smile. "You've come into an unexpected inheritance, and although I have no doubt it doesn't compensate for your ... unfortunate birth circumstance..."

Well, Brette had asked him for forthrightness.

At least he didn't call me a bastard or by-blow to my face.

"No, it doesn't." She'd not pretend it did, either.

Heath patted her hand. "You, unlike many in your situation, have a supportive family and the means to make something of yourself. If I were you, I'd think long and hard on what's truly most important to you."

She gave a reluctant nod.

"If you've wanted to travel, here's your chance, Brette. Perhaps you have a hobby you've wanted to pursue. Well, now you can." Gaze kind, he shook his head. "Don't make any decisions yet. Give yourself time to absorb all of this."

"Indeed, I shall take your advice to heart." And she would, but as wise and kind as Heath was, he couldn't possibly comprehend her internal battle. Brette stood, and the men did too. "I'd like you to continue to investigate whether my parents ever married. If you'd prefer not to, perhaps you can recommend someone who's capable of the task."

Mr. Shipwreck's mouth tipped slightly as he removed his spectacles. "I assure you, it's no problem to have one of my junior clerks do a mite more probing. Honestly, I hope he's able to find a marriage record buried somewhere."

Brette hoped so too, but given her father's reputation, it wasn't blasted likely. Her emotions swung between anger—he'd abandoned her, made no effort to meet her—and gratitude for his neglect, else she wouldn't have known her cousins.

Mr. Shipwreck bade them farewell and retreated to his cluttered desk as she and Heath exited into the chilly outer office. Three clerks scritched away behind high desks, their thin faces creased in concentration. One, sporting a shock of untamed red hair, raised his head, offering a quick smile, and another leveled her a bland glance before they dutifully returned to their work.

The secretary, Mr. Loomis, jumped to his feet and bobbed his head. "Good day to you, sir. Miss."

"Thank you." Heath canted his head. "We can see ourselves out."

What she would do with the money and houses Wiley had settled on her, she'd decide later. "My lord?"

Heath shook his dark head. "We're family now, Brette. When we are alone, it's perfectly acceptable to call me Heath or Raven."

She withdrew the paper Mr. Shipwreck had given her, listing the houses' addresses. "One house is in Kent, but the other is here in London." Perusing the paper again, she wrinkled her brow. "In Belgrave Square." She glanced at him. "Is that a respectable area?"

Were there shops nearby?

"Indeed." Opening the front door, Heath nodded.

London's dankness and pungent smells assailed her, as did the never-ceasing noise.

He closed the door behind them. "It's not an exclusive area, to be sure, Brette, or even high fashion, but certainly genteel. You couldn't live there alone, naturally. That wouldn't be acceptable."

"Of course not." Absorbed in her ruminations, she permitted him to take her elbow and lead her outside. Descending the stairs, she tucked the paper into her reticule, and not attending to where she was going, bumped into a whistling passerby.

"I beg your pardon—" Startled and embarrassed, she met the gentleman's amused emerald eyes. "Alex!"

My, my. So devilishly handsome in his dark blue Garrick coat, a green and gold striped waistcoat peeking from the folds. Evidently tired of black, he'd chosen not to wear mourning attire, and his colorful togs suited him. *My goodness, suits him well, indeed.* She raked her gaze over him, mindful of her pulse's disturbing cavorting.

And here she stood, wearing one of her plainest, most unflattering gowns. At least her pelisse was first rate. The unusual shade, somewhere between sky blue and jade green, flattered her coloring. Or so Brooke had exclaimed when she'd insisted Brette have a pelisse made from the fabric.

Brette returned Alex's infectious grin. She'd not pretend she wasn't thrilled to see him.

"I say, Hawk ... er, Wycombe, it's glad I am to see you looking hale and hearty." Heath and Alex shook hands. "Are you in Town for a few days? Do say you'll come to dinner tonight. I'm sure my lady won't mind."

Alex hesitated, his keen gaze swinging between her and Heath.

"I wish you'd say yes." Brazen as a dockside

whore. But Brette did wish it. She'd missed him awfully. He'd been a constant presence since Heath married Brooke and bundled them off to London.

True, a few days might have gone by without seeing him, but not weeks.

He stepped aside to allow a nurse pushing a pram to bustle past. One eye on the ominous sky, she pulled the blanket higher over her charge. When his gaze encountered Brette's again, a distinct tenderness cradled the corner of his eyes. With what appeared reluctance, he switched his attention to Heath.

A delicious, lovely warmth blossomed in her middle.

"If you're certain it wouldn't be an imposition, and if you'll call me Hawk. Not sure I'll ever get used to the title. I only arrived this afternoon and haven't opened the Berkeley Square house." He shook his head, a half-smile tilting one side of his mouth. "I don't feel I have the right."

"It wouldn't be an inconvenience. Surely you know that." Heath clasped Alex's upper arm. "Why open the house at all? Your rooms at Highfield Place House are untouched, and you're more than welcome to stay with us while you're here."

Brette's stomach fluttered excitedly, and a shiver skittered along her spine. An audacious one she couldn't blame on the brisk, damp wind whipping along the street, scattering the crispy leaves. The sky had taken on a sullen, chain mall hue, guaranteeing rain soon. "Are you walking, Lord Wycombe?"

For a moment, Alex stared at her blankly, a faint flush tinging his angular cheeks. "Forgive me. I didn't realize you were addressing me, Miss Culpepper. But yes, I'm on foot. I needed a spot of air to clear my head."

"Heath, might he ride with us?" She flicked her gloved fingers upward. "I do believe it means to rain."

Another gust blasted into them, and Alex's cologne wafted past. Best dashed smelling man.

A woman could get addicted to his pleasant scent. She eyed him appreciatively. Could get addicted to everything about him, truthfully.

"Of course you must join us. Can we drop you somewhere or will you ride with us to Mayfield?" Heath moved to the carriage where the driver, Peters, stood with the door at the ready.

"No. My business can wait." Alex glanced at the shingle hanging outside the establishment she and Heath had left before following her to the coach. Several other solicitors advertised their vocation along the tidy lane as well.

Their shoulders hunched, the few remaining pedestrians, casting anxious peeks skyward, rushed along, and a man with a brightly colored scarf wound round his neck, his chin tucked to his chest, and his hat drawn low on his head, trotted past on a fine roan.

A landau slowly rolled by, and a young woman's pretty face appeared in the window. One of the Gambwell sisters? Margaret. Catching Brette watching her, she ducked into the vehicle's interior and, a moment later, the shade descended.

First one, then another, fat raindrop splattered onto Brette's bonnet. It would be ruined if she stayed outside, and even though she possessed her own funds now, she disliked wanton waste. "Let's climb into the coach before we're soaked, shall we?"

A few moments later, the pregnant clouds opened up, releasing a deluge. Alex gestured at the onslaught. "Thank you. You saved me from that."

"I ... *We* didn't expect you in the city this soon." Brette dared hope, of course, but he was in mourning and proprieties must be observed.

He and Heath took the opposite seat and relaxed against the pheasant brown squabs. Alex gazed at the passing scenery, unusually subdued and distracted.

"My lord—" Brette ventured.

His mouth quirked again. Most unfair, his being so striking. She couldn't take her gaze from him.

She darted Heath a swift glance. Had he noticed?

No, his attention still centered on Alex.

A gentle smile tipped Alex's mouth. "I'd much prefer you call me Hawk or Alex, as I've asked you before. I don't think Raven will object."

"Yes, but you weren't an earl at that time. It would be most inappropriate, and a woman of my questionable station must behave properly at all times." Rather than chuckle at her quip or respond with a witty remark, he searched her face for a protracted moment.

"You've nothing to be ashamed of. Remember that." Alex returned his focus to the rainy outdoors and his thoughts to whatever had him so thoroughly preoccupied.

Yes, something most definitely wasn't right. Heaviness or despair shrouded the lighthearted man she'd come to know these past months.

Brette cast Heath a questioning look.

He'd detected it too. "Hawk, we've been friends for two decades, and I recognize that glum expression. What's wrong?"

Alex lifted a shoulder slightly, his gaze yet riveted on the bleak scenery. "I'm afraid there's ugly speculation that Wycombe's and his son's deaths weren't an accident. That the fire was set deliberately."

Brette gasped and clapped her hand to her mouth.

"By God, never say so." Heath pounded his thigh.

"Do the authorities suspect someone?" Alex ceased perusing the deserted street, and his tormented gaze meshed with hers.

Oh, my God.

Disquiet haunting his beautiful green eyes, his voice the merest shred, he murmured, "Me."

B rette kicked at the leaves dusting the Hyde Park walking path. Yesterday afternoon's rainstorm had shaken myriads loose, and a colorful, soggy quilt covered the ground. Puddles pooled here and there, despite the brightly shining sun. The golden rays failed to warm the air, however, and a nippy breeze chilled her face.

She'd forgotten her handkerchief, and the cold made her nose run. She sniffed loudly, kicking another bunch of leaves.

Unfair. So blasted unfair.

How could anyone suspect Alex of such grotesque crimes as arson and murder? He'd assured her and Heath he had an alibi, but strain, nevertheless, marked his features. How could it not until he'd been vindicated?

A few feet away, a scolding squirrel scampered up a tree and Brooke, strolling with Heath behind Brette, laughed. A trifle wan, Brooke had dared a short walk today. The fresh air would benefit her. The babe too.

Brette couldn't decide if she wanted a niece or a nephew. She planned on spoiling the darling no matter the infant's sex. Spinster aunts were permitted the luxury. Her musings turned to last night. Dinner had passed pleasantly enough, but the undercurrent of Alex's disconcerting revelation had kept the mood somber. He'd departed the house early this morning, leaving word with Jenkin he'd be gone the entire day.

Drat it all.

Brette shouldn't have been disappointed. They were merely friends, and couldn't be anything more. That truth shouldn't have bothered so much. But it did, nonetheless.

An unkind giggle drew her from her musings.

The three Gambwell sisters and their severe mother approached from the opposite direction. The fair weather had lured many outdoors this morning, including unpleasant creatures normally hiding beneath rocks or staying abed until noon.

Margaret Gambwell pointed at Brette and whispered, sotto voce, in Charlotte's ear. "Isn't Bret a man's name?"

Both erupted into gales of laughter while the third and youngest sister, Harriot, coldly stared at Brette.

Third time this week.

She could expect more of the same. Mayhap tomorrow, she'd take her constitutional in The Green Park.

Brette refused to slow her stride or shirk away. Head held high, she continued on, but as she passed the tittering misses, the dame lifted her nose as if she smelled something foul, pointed her haughty gaze skyward, and yanked her skirts aside. The younger women immediately followed suit.

The cut sublime.

An anger-borne flush heated Brette's cheeks, but she braced her shoulders and slanted her head politely. She'd not degrade herself and respond in kind, though she itched to give the pompous quartet a piece of her mind.

"There you are, Miss Culpepper," Alex called, waving his hand and looking exceedingly dashing in a Spanish brown greatcoat. He held a puppy clasped in his other arm. "Please forgive me for my tardiness. I'm afraid Domino here escaped me, and I was forced to chase the rascally whelp."

Impeccable timing. Brette couldn't prevent her

overjoyed smile. "Lord Wycombe."

At the envious pouts turning down the sisters' mouths, and the peeved scowl twitching Lady Gambwell's unnaturally dark eyebrows, Brette's smile may have taken on a gloating mien. But only the merest touch. Never anything as vulgar as outright jubilation.

As Brooke and Heath reached her, ready to do battle—she guessed from the displeased expressions tightening their faces—Alex strode to her side and graced her with a rakish smile.

Good Lord.

When he smiled so roguishly, her muddled thoughts refused to order themselves.

The Gambwells seemed similarly afflicted. They stood, gaping like besotted or inebriated nincompoops. Even the married elder.

"Good day to you, Lady Gambwell." He politely doffed his hat while trying to subdue the wriggling mass of black and white he held with a tongue determined to sample Alex's chin and cheeks. "Miss Gambwell. Miss Charlotte. Miss Margar—"

The pup's pink tongue slipped between his lips, and Alex laughed as he attempted to rearrange the excited dog. "Behave, Domino."

"My dear Lord Wycombe," simpered Lady Gambwell, her husband-hunting teeth bared in what she no doubt presumed a smile. A hyena's evil grin right before it attacked its prey. She flapped her purple-gloved hand at her ogling offspring. "You remember my daughters, of course. Girls, curtsy."

Brette raised a skeptical brow.

Is she daft? Of course he remembers. He just greeted them by name.

Like puppets, the trio bobbed their bonneted heads and batted their suspiciously dark eyelashes. A little bee's wax and soot perhaps? Lip rouge too, or Brette hadn't eaten kippers for breakfast.

Careful to keep Domino pointed away from his face, Alex flashed his white teeth again and played the gallant. "How could I possibly forget? You faithfully attended St. Peter's."

Every. Last. Sunday. Sitting in the front pew.

Bosoms displayed like a baker's quarter loafs.

Brette eyeballed their chests. Well, maybe more like dinner rolls. *That failed to rise sufficiently.* Her gaze slid to sixteen-year-old Harriot's flat-as-an-oatcake bosom. *Or at all.*

The Gambwell sisters brazenly simpered and posed, each seemingly determined to draw his attention to them with their wanton antics.

What a ridiculous display. Brette barely kept from rolling her eyes, and instead rubbed behind the pup's one white and one black ear. Alex hadn't been prestigious enough for them as a rector, but as an earl, he'd become the title-hungry cabbage-heads' quarry.

"Who do you have here?" Brette stroked the puppy's spine. She giggled when he flopped backward in Alex's arms, his fat puppy paws in the air, in an attempt to slather her with slobbery canine kisses.

"This would be Domino." Alex bent and placed the rambunctious dog on the pathway.

Domino immediately lunged for the squirrel gathering acorns beneath a nearby oak. His lead brought him up short, but the inconvenience didn't stop the spirited dog from yapping and straining against the leash.

"Lord and Lady Ravensdale." Lady Gambwell finally acknowledged Brooke and Heath. And pointedly ignored Brette.

Last spring, Brette had sat in several drawing rooms, enjoying tea with one or more of the Gambwells, and today, they treated her as if she were fresh horse droppings.

Neither Brooke nor Heath returned her ladyship's forced greeting, just coolly inclined their heads. Pity they possessed too much decency to cut Lady Gambwell and her tittering daughters dead.

"Come along, Brette. I grow fatigued and chilled."

Brooke clasped her arm and bestowed a benevolent smile on Alex. "Your tardiness is forgiven, Lord Wycombe, since I cannot remain miffed at my husband's *dearest* friend and our *honored* houseguest."

Oh, bravo, Brooke. Well done, you.

Lady Gambwell made an inarticulate sound, and her face turned an unbecoming puce shade, as if she'd been served a long dead reptile at tea instead of dainties and sweets.

Brette arced a brow and graced him with what she hoped was her sweetest, most flirtatious smile. She normally didn't stoop to low behavior, but for the Gambwells, she'd gladly make the descent this once. "I too forgive you, Alex." Yes, she dared use his given name. Scandalous. "But only if you promise we might venture to Egyptian Hall to view the Laplander exhibition that I've heard everyone singing the praises of."

How's that for bold? Was the exhibition even open in October?

The answering gleam in his eyes told her he knew her game. "It would be my utmost pleasure, Miss Culpepper. I believe they offer sleigh or sled rides too. And of course, I insist that you permit me to take you for a chocolate afterward." He touched his hat's brim. "Ladies."

He effectively dismissed the Gambwells, and they'd no choice but to step aside and allow Brette and the others to continue on their way.

After they'd put distance between themselves and the disgruntled foursome, Brette tapped his arm and chuckled naughtily. "Did you catch their expressions when they learned you stay at Highfield Place House with us, my lord? Or when I used your given name?"

"Indeed. Looked like they'd taken a swig of unsweetened lemonade." His chuckle was every bit as mischievous as hers. "I was able to conclude my business earlier than anticipated, so I collected Domino from the stables where I'd left him yesterday."

Hearing his name, the puppy reared onto his haunches while scratching at Alex's leg. "Down, Domino," Alex admonished firmly but gently.

Alex fell in step beside Heath.

"I hope you don't mind if the puppy stays at the house." Alex struggled to contain the excited dog, weaving between their legs. "If he'll be an inconvenience, I can take him to the stables, though the stable master was in a sour mood after this chap chewed a harness and a grooming brush."

"Freddy will enjoy his company, I think." Brooke gave the high-spirited pup a tolerant smile. "It would do Freddy good to play. He needs the exercise. He's far too fat."

"Yes, but that would require him to move." Brette's droll observation earned her smiles all around.

"Keep him away from my boots is all I ask." Heath chuckled and scooped to scratch Domino's ears. The pup tried to snatch his fingers. Heath straightened, his features serious. "How went your meeting?"

So he knew where Alex had gamboled off to before breakfast.

"Well enough, I suppose. I gave my solicitor the names of the family I dined with the evening Charlbury burned, and they'll be contacted to verify I was with them. Also, given I was in London, and Charlbury Lodge is four hours' hard ride from here, I didn't have enough time to ride there and preside over the Holy Eucharist Sunday morning at eight o'clock. My housekeeper can testify that I arose at half past five that morning, as well."

Hardly an extended arm's length separated Brette and Brooke from the Alex and Heath following them. The men spoke softly, though not secretly, but Alex didn't sound completely convinced to Brette. She slowed her steps, and when the men came abreast, Brooke took Heath's arm.

Brette cut Alex a sidelong glance.

He wouldn't admit it, not to them, but his cheerful

demeanor didn't completely hide the disquiet in his eyes.

"Until the matter is completely settled, and until I have the name of who dared accuse me of the foulness, I cannot relax." Alex extended his free elbow to Brette. "I can, however, try to escort you, though with this unruly fellow, I cannot guarantee we won't be tripped."

"I'll take my chances." Any chance to touch him at all. She slipped her hand into the crook.

He tucked his arm close to his side, the movement so natural, she couldn't object. Even if keeping his balance and controlling the dog cavorting at the end of the leash motivated him, rather than an intention to be nearer her.

Walking with him, their arms entwined, and the pup pulling at his leash seemed almost domesticated. Her heart gave its own disjointed tug.

Dangerous, entertaining, fanciful notions.

A leaf tumbled past, and the pup pounced on it.

Alex's forearm flexed, and he instinctively hugged her hand nearer his side.

She couldn't detect an ounce of fat on either his solid arm or firm ribs. Brette laughed as Domino seized the leaf in his mouth, shaking his head and growling. "I think you're going to have your hands full with him."

"Most assuredly. But I've always wanted my own

dog. The countess was none too pleased when I brought Domino into High Wycombe, I can tell you. But she'll be leaving shortly and couldn't kick up too much fuss."

"So what happens now? Once your name is cleared, what will you do first?" They'd fallen several paces behind Brooke and Heath.

"I haven't decided. Wycombe neglected the estate, and her finances are in a deplorable state. I suppose I'll start there, and worry about the rest as it arises." He contracted his arm. "How are you? I've been concerned. Has anyone treated you poorly? I'll give them an earful on the pitfalls of a judgmental spirit."

Such earnestness. Brette couldn't deny she enjoyed his protectiveness. "It's expected. Silly though it might be, I'm hopeful a marriage record for my parents might be found. Are you familiar with Fusty Boots, the Duke of Bellinghamshire?"

"I never met the fellow, but I've heard of him. A cantankerous curmudgeon, famous for his foul-smelling feet, so malodorous even his boots couldn't contain the stink. I believe he died a few years past. Why?" Alex twisted his other hand, wrapping the leather lead a few times around it. Domino wasn't pleased by his shortened leash and renewed his efforts to chase anything that moved.

"Supposedly, he was my grandfather, and from

your description, I'm not altogether certain that's a good thing. Do you suppose his feet truly smelled so dreadful?"

Heath threw a knowing glance over his shoulder and gave a crisp nod. "Worse. I sat near him once at dinner. Could barely get my food down, and when the fish was served ... God's toenails."

At his unintended joke, they burst into laughter.

A swaggering grin tipping his lips, Alex eyed her square-toed half boots.

Brette poked his shoulder. "Don't you dare suggest anything so ungentlemanly."

They arrived at Highland Park House, and a few minutes later the four assembled in the drawing room, less one sleepy, dappled pup. After depositing a fresh tea tray on the oval table between the burgundy and gold striped silk settees, Jenkin had bidden a footman take the spotted tornado to the kitchen for a snack and a nap.

Brooke, a trifle pale, delicate lines of weariness etching her forehead, sank into the chair nearest the toasty fire. "Brette, dear, would you pour. I'm afraid I feel a trifle unwell."

At once all solicitousness, Heath drew another chair beside hers and took her hand. "Perhaps you should have a rest."

"We'll see, darling. I'm fine for the present." Ah,

because dear Brooke didn't want to leave Alex and Brette alone? Did she worry about more tattle?

Brette prepared each cup—two lumps, no cream for Alex—and expertly poured the fragrant tea. After handing everyone their teacup, she motioned to the plate of sweets. "I tried my hand at a new delicacy. It's Scottish black bun, a pastry-covered fruit cake."

"No, thank you. Just tea for me." Did Brooke's tummy trouble her again? This pregnancy business wasn't all the crack.

Alex and Heath each added several treats to their plates. You'd have assumed they'd walked for miles from the way they dug into the pastries and cakes.

A grin wreathed Alex's face as he forked a piece of the black bun. "One of my favorites." He sank his teeth into the flakiness, his brows vaulting to his hairline. "You made this? It's excellent."

"Thank you." His earnest compliment sent heat skittering across Brette's cheeks. "And, yes, I made it a couple of weeks ago. It has to age to reach its full potential. I do like baking though. I might use my inheritance to open a pastry shop."

There. She'd said it.

Three startled gazes snapped to her, yet not one of them objected. *Hmm*, they'd already concluded her prospects were that dismal that she'd need an occupation? Rather disheartening.

The future she'd intended had taken an abrupt turn, and at twenty, Brette couldn't decide which of the limited pathways before her she should take. So much for being the author of her own destiny.

Lips thinned, Brooke pressed her hand to her waist. She truly must not be feeling well.

However, after a deep breath, which she held for a moment before slowly releasing, she perked up. "Oh, I almost forgot. The Goodinghams have invited us for dinner three nights hence. Nothing too terribly large or formal, I don't believe. A dozen guests in all with dancing afterward. Mrs. Goodingham mentioned they're one male short. Shall I tell her you will join us, Hawk?"

Brette's stomach sank to her damp boots. Who else had received a dinner invitation? She hadn't cared before, but the line was slowing emerging between those who intended to shun her and those who would continue to acknowledge and welcome her.

Utter drivel.

She had no control over her birth. It didn't affect her character or worthiness.

As much as she'd enjoyed London and the Season's frenzy, the more staid, less formal country life offered something too. Specifically, the welcome lack of pompous busybodies determining who met the mark and who they deemed beneath their touch.

Brooke chuckled. "I'm still not accustomed to your title, Wycombe."

"I'd be honored to attend, and you can still call me Hawk, if you wish." Alex replaced the snuff box he'd been admiring. "This is new, Raven. How many do you have now?" Alex's mouth moved as he silently counted the boxes displayed on a corner shelf. "Seven-and-twenty. And you've never used snuff."

"I can appreciate beauty, no matter its form." Heath's regard rested on Brooke.

"I'll send a note round this afternoon and tell Mrs. Goodhingham you've agreed to join us, Wycombe." Brooke straightened, her face distressed, and her eyes darkened to midnight blue. "Please excuse me. I'm not feeling well." She clasped Heath's arm. "Would you please assist me to our chamber? I need to lie down."

At once, Brette, Heath, and Alex jumped to their feet.

Heath helped Brooke stand, but instead of wrapping an arm about her thickening waist, he scooped her into his arms.

"This isn't necessary. I can walk." She laid her head against his chest despite her mild protest.

"It most certainly is, and you cannot. I'll not have

you risking a tumble." Heath jerked his head toward the entrance. "Hawk, the door please."

Alex hurried to do his bidding, and after they'd stepped into the corridor, he stood sideway in the doorway, hands on his hips, his face taut with concern.

Brette had found him attractive in his staid black, but today, wearing a charcoal-collared hunter green cutaway which emphasized his broad shoulders—how could she not have noticed their breadth before?—buff pantaloons that did his muscled thighs credit, and a daring navy and jade, silver-threaded waistcoat... Well, dragging her gaze from him took colossal effort.

She admired him from beneath her lashes, taking in his patrician profile.

Better find something to do, lest he catch her ogling him. An undesirable shouldn't daydream about an earl. She lifted the brass poker. Ladies didn't attend to their own fire, but having lived a life of poverty at Esherton Green, none of the Culpepper misses put on airs.

Crouching, she prodded the logs then glanced over her shoulder when he continued to remain silent.

He finally swiveled to face her. "How could something as wonderful as carrying a child cause such discomfort?" Sighing, he cupped his nape, disturbing the curls scraping his collar. "Another reason I wasn't equipped for the Church."

Alex's decency far surpassed every man's she knew, Heath and Leventhorpe included. She adored them both now—the big, over-protective gollumpuses—but initially, they'd kept their positive qualities hidden beneath spikey exteriors.

Alex, on the other hand, couldn't have been more transparent.

She canted her head. "Oh? Why do you think you weren't meant for the Church? I disagree. I think you proved yourself an admirable rector."

He lifted a small, framed portrait and examined the likeness. "I questioned—still question—God's design and my purpose. Regularly."

"But, don't we all, at times?" Returning her attention to the fire, she gave the logs an exuberant poke, sending sparks exploding up the chimney.

At the swish behind her, she cast him a startled glance. He'd silently crossed the room and stood a mere foot away.

Leisurely and most enjoyably, she permitted her gaze to climb his thighs, past his trim hips and slender waist, over his chest's broad swell and his cleverly knotted cravat, to his chiseled jaw, and, lastly, his molded mouth.

He extended a hand, but the simple gesture meant much more.

Silently, he beckoned her, and she couldn't refuse his summons any more than a bird voluntarily stopped flying. Their nature compelled them to take wing just as her heart—her gullible, imprudent heart—urged her to answer his winsome command.

She placed her palm in his, welcoming the warm, firm grip, and the delicious tremor shaking her. Slowly uncurling from her squat, she raised her eyes, and the tenderness gleaming in his warmed her blood and her bones to their marrow.

As he cupped her shoulders, drawing her near, the poker slid from her fingers, clanking noisily onto the marble hearth.

"Brette...?"

One syllable, a sensual, throaty, verbal caress. An irresistible snare she'd gladly walk into.

He framed her jaw with his forefinger and thumb, rubbing the bone gently. "I want to kiss you."

"I know." She wanted to kiss him too.

Brette raised onto her toes. How else could their lips possibly meet? Him so tall and she not the least? She must make him understand she welcomed his kiss; he'd never take advantage otherwise. And she did so want his mouth on hers.

So very much. Right or wrong.

Stretching, she arched into him, deliciously,

gratifyingly, from hip to breast. Arms looped around his strong neck, she slanted her head and offered him her mouth.

He encircled her, wrapping his arms around her back, his fingers splayed against her sides, and brought his mouth to hers.

A blissful sigh escaped her, followed by a gasp of pleasure when Alex teased her lips apart with his tongue. Her senses came alive, melding into one riotous sensation as his raspy breaths joined with hers. His unique scent, his taste upon her tongue, his hard, rippling muscles beneath her fingertips, and his firm yet velvety mouth moving upon hers engulfed her in the headiest of sensations, as if she floated.

"Ahem."

A prudent woman knows 'tis
better to have no money but a pure
heart than to be rich with bad intentions.
*~Appearances and Attitude—The Genteel Lady's
Guide to Practical Living*

Alex plummeted to earth as a clearly exasperated male cleared his throat again.

"*Aa-hemm!*" Raven's irritated voice cooled Alex's ardor faster than a February dip in the Thames.

He and Brette looked—*were*—guilty as hell.

And yet, he didn't want to release her, to let the enchantment they'd shared go. Her tantalizing perfume still teased his senses, and as he'd kissed her, several strands of her silky hair had escaped their pins, one coiling around the wrist of the hand cradling her head.

He locked his legs as she wobbled, and only his arms encircling her kept her from toppling.

Want sluiced through him again. Best change his musings before Raven called him out.

"Dear me," Brette whispered, huskily into Alex's

shoulder, as she clutched his lapels.

Panting softly, her gently sloping cheeks nearly the same hue as her soft pink gown, she leaned heavily against him, as unbalanced as he.

She'd tilted his senses, his carefully ordered world right off its axis.

He hadn't a great deal of carnal practice, despite women boldly offering themselves on a regular basis, including former parishioners. But what he'd just experienced with Brette... Mere words couldn't do it justice.

The doorway framed Raven, his legs braced and arms folded. The stance of an outraged guardian. The darkling look he speared Alex made his scalp tingle. Alex had breached an unspoken rule between the five rogues, and Raven wouldn't pardon him readily.

"Why do I continually find my wards in compromising situations with my closest friends? First Trist with Blythe and now you with Brette. It's enough to make me want to trot the girls off to a convent in France." Raven rolled his eyes, but an instant later froze, horror-struck, his arms falling to his sides. He took a couple of uncertain steps. "Blister and damn. Drake and Whitehouse hadn't better look at the twins with anything more than decrepit, grandfatherly attention or I'll—"

Alex released a short laugh and stepped away from Brette, though he kept his hand at her elbow to steady her. "My dear chap. That ship has sailed. Quite literally. How, pray tell, will *you* do anything? Did you seriously not consider the possibility?"

Given the green tinge about Raven's mouth, Alex almost regretted gibing him. Almost.

Alex had detected the covert, and not so covert, looks Drake and Whitehouse gave Blaire and Blaike. And neither of the chaps claimed the degree of gentlemanliness Raven, Leventhorpe, or he did. He'd not voice *those* disconcerting musings, though. Raven couldn't leave his *enceinte* wife to trundle after his wards.

Besides, the damage might already have been done. The twins and their chaperone had sailed weeks ago. Probably no need to worry in any event. Drake and Whitehouse weren't complete and utter scoundrels. *Usually.*

Brette drew in a weighty breath and, her color high, scooted away from Alex. "The girls aren't without common sense. I'd not worry yourself overly much on their account, Heath. And Mrs. Hobbs is a dragon, a true paragon of virtue. Anyone who as much as looks at either twin without proper respect will be whacked soundly upon his nog."

True. The first time Alex laid eyes on the granite-faced dame, he'd winced at her formidable countenance and half expected her to breathe fire when she opened her mouth to speak.

Scowling, Raven stalked to them, his gaze swinging between Brette and Alex the whole while as if trying to read their minds.

He took his guardianship seriously, and Alex respected him for it. Nonetheless, he didn't relish losing one of his dearest chums over a stolen kiss.

Far more than that, and you know it. It can't be. Not yet.

He'd offer for Brette in an instant, but not *this* precise instant.

Not until he'd settled the suspicious fire business, and he could guarantee her safety. And not until he knew the financial status of his estate. He must be able to offer her more than a mere title, a manor in dire need of renovation, and a few scrawny sheep.

A mere title?

How virtuous he sounded. Alex smothered his snort of laughter.

"Be that as it may, explain yourself, Hawk. I'd have expected unacceptable behavior from any of the others, but not from you."

"Why? Because, until a few weeks ago, I called

myself a man of God and practiced a wholly different profession? You, of all people, know I didn't seek the position, any more than I sought a title, though I gave the Church my best. I've never professed to be a saint." Alex straightened his rumpled waistcoat, keeping one eye on Brette as she tidied the tea tray.

He'd be bound chagrin prompted her actions more than a desire to help the efficient staff. Did she regret their kiss?

She lifted a plate of dainties and smiling, offered Heath one. "Sweet, Heath?" A diversion?

"What I want to know is what do you intend to do about it?" Raven absently selected the nearest sweetmeat, his unrelenting gaze demanding an answer from Alex.

Raven popped the bonbon into his mouth and immediately grimaced. He managed to chew and swallow the confection before seizing a cup of cold tea and gulping it down. "What in God's name *was* that?"

Alex bit back another laugh, grateful Brette's tactic had worked.

Picking up a serviette, her expression the epitome of innocence, Brette glanced at the plate. "I think it was an almond liqueur filled bonbon."

Clever minx.

Raven might be annoyed that Alex had overstepped

the bounds, but he'd approve the match despite his obligatory fussing. A respectable guardian must bluster a mite, and Raven couldn't appear too pleased at the turn of events. He'd feel guilty if he did, as if he hadn't done his duty by Brette.

"I expect you've already proposed. I must say it's high-handed of you, Hawk, not speaking with me first to ask for Brette's hand." Raven wiped his sticky fingers on a serviette.

Devil take it.

Naturally, he would jump to that unfortunate and inaccurate conclusion.

Brette dropped a cup, the shattering china clanging loudly in the silent room as fragments and biscuits scattered across the table and onto the floor. Fetching eyes wide in her perfect oval face, her gaze whipped to Raven then to Alex then back to Raven. "You think—?"

Freddy tottered into the drawing room and, sniffing loudly, made straight for the tea table.

"No, Freddy, you'll cut yourself." Brette rushed to intercept the dog. Gathering him in her arms, she shook her hair from her face and shoulder.

The loose tendrils caressed her cheek, and Alex half-lifted his hand to smooth the moonstruck tresses behind her ear before he caught himself.

"I'm afraid you're mistaken, Heath. There will be no match between Lord Wycombe and myself." She nuzzled Freddy's fat neck. To hide her face?

"Why not?" It did rather smart Alex's pride. Refused before he'd proposed. He was an earl, after all. And he loved her.

Stow it.

A moment ago, he'd been listing the reasons he couldn't marry her

Yet.

Raven blinked, his face a comical mixture of disbelief and astonishment. "Yes, do tell, why not?"

Another time, Alex might have snickered at his friend's bafflement, but not when he reeled from her response himself.

Back half-turned to him, Brette kissed Freddy's tawny head. "Until my circumstances—"

A rather flustered Jenkin loomed in the doorway. "Sir, the Dowager Countess of Wycombe has called. I've asked her to wait in the entry while I inquire if anyone is at home to receive her."

His mien very much suggested he hoped Raven would say no.

Alex sorely wished he would. Grandmother or not, the cagey old bat, couldn't be up to any good.

"Of course they are, you numbskull. I can hear

them babbling nonsensical balderdash about my grandson marrying an unsuitable chit." A cane rapped Jenkin's calf. "Move aside, man."

Brette's mouth parted, and she slung Alex an appalled glance.

Wearing an oversized purple bonnet, weighted with enough plumage to cover an ostrich's arse, Grandmama sailed into the drawing room. She banged her cane raucously with each uneven step.

"Lady Gambwell mentioned you were in Town, Wycombe." Her critical gaze disdainfully swept the room and its occupants. "Though why you've chosen to stay *here* rather than at your residence or with me, I cannot begin to fathom."

For the first time in all the years Alex had known him, Jenkin gaped, speechless. He could hardly haul the dowager from the room, though given his slightly narrowed eyes and elevated brows, the notion had crossed the majordomo's mind.

"Give me a kiss, boy." Grandmama presented her crepey cheek.

A kiss? She wanted a kiss? From Alex? First time for everything.

He dropped a peck on her cool skin. Well, at least he hadn't turned to stone. Or ice. "To what do I owe this unexpected *pleasure*?"

"*Hmph.* You don't fool me, insolent pup. I know you aren't happy I called." She thumped her cane for emphasis, and Freddy buried his head in Brette's shoulder.

Visions of leeches, bloodletting cups, and medieval torture devices popped into Alex's mind. He would've welcomed every single one more than Grandmama.

She hadn't ever a kind or gentle word for him. Not when he'd been a child, and she called him a weak, mewling milksop, and certainly not after he reached adulthood. All her devotion and attention she'd directed to the heir, Arthur, and when poor Lawrence came along, she'd dug her talons into him.

Squinting, her gaze raking him from toe to top, her mouth swept down impossibly further. "Why aren't you wearing black? Have you no respect for your cousins? Is this what's become of associating with riffraff and scallywags?"

"As a rector, I hardly associated with undesirables." The downcast and unfortunate, certainly. Such compassion proved beyond her scope of understanding, however.

She hadn't expected an answer, and from her thinned mouth, didn't like his. She never did. Just criticized and complained and made everyone within hearing distance wish to be somewhere else. Anywhere else.

Alex angled his head and extended his arm. "Please allow me to introduce Heath, the Earl of Ravensdale and his ward, Miss Brette Culpepper."

"Bah, don't waste my time with trivialities." Grandmama turned her critical regard on Brette, a slight sneer on her thin lips, before her arctic gaze gravitated to Alex. Using both hands, she rammed her cane into the unfortunate floor once more. "Do you honestly think to tarnish the earldom or our family name by marrying a common bastard?"

Alex stiffened. "That's outside of enough!"

"I." *Wham.* "Won't." *Wham.* "Allow." *Wham.* "It." *Wham.* The china on the tea tray rattled with each angry blow of her cane.

Her blood thrumming with ire, Brette shifted a cowering Freddy higher in her arms. Convenient she held the nervous dog or, for the first time in her life, she might have slapped another woman's face. Elderly or not.

If Freddy had possessed more than a half dozen teeth, and Brette hadn't been afraid he'd promptly die from the toxins, she would've set him on the hateful dame.

"You have no say in what I do, Grandmama, and if you think I'll permit you to disparage Miss Culpepper, you are gravely mistaken. Apologize."

His grandmother angled her head loftily, the feathers adorning her hat, jerking with the sudden movement. "I shall not. She is beneath me."

Brette had never seen Alex this furious—his square chin set determinedly and his gaze inflexible—and though a prudent woman would've ignored the dowager's rudeness, Brette hurled common sense aside. After all, what did she have to lose?

"Better to claim humble origins and demonstrate kindness and integrity than be highborn without a shred of decency or compassion." She arched a brow and lifted her chin in a challenge. "Or have an elevated sense of one's worth."

Heath's mouth twitched before he brought the quivering flesh under control.

The dowager shook her cane at Brette, coming perilously close to striking her. "Precisely the kind of impudent hogwash I'd expect from a wench of your ilk. That's what comes of being raised with bovines. No breeding or refinement. Common riffraff."

Freddy growled a warning low in his throat.

"You go too far." Alex stepped forward, and his

grandmother whopped his leg with her cane. He grabbed the offended calf. "Ouch."

"Wycombe, collect your effects. We're leaving at once. I won't spend another moment in the presence of this ... this undesirable." She brandished the walking stick again, and the urge to yank the menace from the grand dame's arthritis twisted fingers tempted Brette unmercifully.

"Madam, in my home, you will not speak with such disrespect, particularly to my ward." Heath stepped beside Brette in an obvious protective gesture.

Alex limped to her other side.

Two champions. Three, if you counted Freddy's sporadic rumbles. Her heart swelled with appreciation and something much more powerful.

"I am not leaving, Grandmama, and you *will* apologize for your reprehensible rudeness to Miss Culpepper. She is the granddaughter of the Duke of Bellinghamshire, and claims both Spanish and Scandinavian royalty in her lineage. She possesses more blue-blood than you or I. Or have you conveniently forgotten *your* origins?"

The dowager opened her mouth, no doubt ready to deliver a spicy retort, but Alex's stern look muted her. Her savage tongue at least. Her eyes continued a reproachful monologue.

He flicked a forefinger at his grandmother's inflexible expression. "If I recall, we've a commoner or two," he raised another finger, "a traitor, a horse thief, oh, and a ... *courtesan* dangling from various branches of our family's tree."

He wiggled his splayed fingers, and Brette caught the inside of her cheek between her teeth to keep from giggling as the dowager's eyes narrowed further with each unacceptable person he mentioned.

"I'm sure I have no idea to what you're mistakenly referring." The dowager managed to scornfully peer down her nose at her grandson, though he stood a full foot taller. "A courtesan, indeed. Balderdash. Nonsensical twaddle." She sniffed, disdain oozing from her.

"We both know the term is most benevolent, but I strove for discretion, regarding my two times Great Aunt Ruby. Your mother's sister, wasn't she, Grandmama?"

Brette swung her startled gaze to Alex. "A courtesan? Truly? I must hear the tale. And however did you learn about my pedigree?"

His mouth kicked up on one side. "For months, I've listened to Raven and Leventhorpe extol the virtues of two other Culpepper misses."

"So, you intend to defy me?" The dowager

completely ignored his references to her dubious relative.

Alex's features softened. "I intend to do what's right and honorable."

"You're a pudding soft fool, Wycombe." Scathing disapproval pinching her features, she shook her head, sending her bonnet's feathers to bouncing one more. "I'm not giving up the field just yet. You wait and see."

Big surprise there.

Heath canted his head, just this side of civil. "Jenkin, please escort the Dowager Countess out."

"With utmost pleasure, sir." Hand on the door, Jenkin stared down the length of his considerable nose. "Madame, if you please?"

And even if she doesn't.

Giving Brette a final haughty glare, the dowager stalked from the room, her cane hammering the floor with each vexed step.

Brette released her pent-up breath. More than a mite disconcerting, being thoroughly disliked by someone she'd just met. "I've the beginnings of a headache." Worsened by the continued pounding of the Dowager Countess Wycombe's sorely abused cane. "And I wish to look in on Brooke as well. If you'll excuse me?"

"In a moment." Heath's raised hand detained her.

Oh, bother.

"We haven't finished our earlier discussion."

Yes. We have.

Usually stoic, he rubbed his knitted brow above his left eye. Likely a drum echoed within his skull too. "Are you or are you not betrothed?"

His question included Alex.

"We are not." If only it were possible. It galled her to admit it, but the dowager was right.

Brette couldn't ask Alex to disgrace the earldom by joining with a by-blow. No evidence existed that proved otherwise, and until it did—*if* it ever did—she'd have to endure the shame. She couldn't ask him to do the same.

Alex dared to finger a wayward curl before looping it behind her ear, staring straight into her soul, his expression so tender, she wanted to weep.

I can't, Alex. Please don't ask me.

"We could be, Brette. In time. After I've put my affairs in order and cleared my name. I'd be honored above all else, if you'd have me."

9

From beneath hooded eyes, primal appreciation warming his blood, Alex regarded Brette as the carriage gently swayed. She and Lady Ravensdale spoke quietly about a blanket Brette was crocheting for the babe.

He'd tried to cry off attending the Goodinghams' dinner party, but Brooke had gently reminded him she'd already sent an acceptance on his behalf. If he wasn't prostrate in bed, *dying,* his absence would reflect poorly on them. Something they tried to avoid presently.

The exaggeration hadn't been lost on him, but he'd taken her point.

They couldn't risk offending those still welcoming Brette into their exclusive parlors. The others were a bunch of pompous windbags, most with a secret or two *or twenty* they wouldn't appreciate bandied about publically. As rector, he'd been privy to more than one guilty confession which made their treatment of Brette harder to stomach.

No oath prevented him from sharing those tidbits now, but his conscience did, blister it.

He covered his mouth with a forefinger, curbing his burgeoning smile. Permitted uncharitable opinions without immediate self-recrimination. How refreshing.

A smile lit Brette's face as she laughed at something her sister, er, cousin said, her unreserved joy adding to her already staggering exquisiteness.

His breath had left him in a gut-punching whoosh when she'd descended the stairs tonight, absolutely ravishing in a sapphire and white gown embellished with silver threads and lace, her glorious halo of moon spun hair twisted into a new and most becoming style, complete with a jeweled circlet sparkling between the shiny tendrils.

Up to now, he'd attributed such sentimental fribble to enamored—or drunken—corkbrains, but when he'd tried to draw in a meager breath and his blasted lungs refused to cooperate, he could no longer deny the phenomenon existed.

How could she possibly have grown more beautiful

since yesterday? How could he have become more besotted?

The carriage sank into a bone-jarring rut, nearly vaulting him from his seat. His foot accidently brushed her skirt before he retreated into the coach's shadows once more.

Bestowing him a forgiving smile, her gaze genial, yet slightly hesitant around the edges, she searched his face. When he didn't respond with an upward sweep of his lips, she dropped her gaze and captured her plump lower lip between her teeth.

He'd nibbled that tasty spot of wonderfulness only yesterday. Was she recalling their kiss as well?

Or his botched declaration?

Two proposals and two refusals. Rather bruised his pride, it did.

Why had she rejected him again?

Rubbing his gloved fingers together, he pulled his eyebrows tight. Perhaps she fancied another, unbeknownst to him. Why hadn't that occurred to him before? If so, who was the chap?

Did it matter?

A third proposal wouldn't be forthcoming. The iota of pride he hadn't surrendered while rector demanded he not make himself an idiot over her again.

He'd actually believed she might accept his

spontaneous offer this time, if he assured her they'd wait to marry. After all, he wasn't in a position to wed yet, but he'd wanted to claim her as his own, declare to the world she was his. More fool he. Bad enough if they'd been alone, but he'd plunged common sense into the ocean's depths and asked with an audience. Again.

Raven hadn't broached the subject since. Good friend there. Responsible guardian, too.

Would he ask Alex to leave Highfield now? To spare Brette the awkwardness his presence caused?

Alex had half-expected a summons today, requesting he remove himself to his townhouse.

Instead, Raven had invited Alex to join him at White's and studiously avoided mention of yesterday's farce, directing their conversation to Tattersall's next auction instead.

Ten minutes later, the foursome mingled in the Goodninghams' gold salon, awaiting the final guests' arrival. The dinner party, nineteen thus far, might have been bearable if Lord and Lady Gambwell and their eldest daughters, Margaret and Charlotte, weren't also in attendance. Their eyes brightened like Vauxhall Garden fireworks when they'd spotted him.

He'd almost pivoted and marched to the coach, but Brette's tiny, startled, despairing gasp had set his feet advancing instead. Her adorable chin inched upward, and she pasted a pleasant look upon her face. He'd be bound she'd gnaw her beaded slippers before she let those chits grasp how they affected her.

He would too, by George.

Miss Gambwell, arching her neck to display the length to her best advantage, ran her fingers across the harpsichord's ivory keyboard, all the while giving him a coy look. "I do hope we'll have the opportunity to sing and ... *play* together after dinner."

Well, that's as subtle as an orange pig.

Standing to Alex's left, near a large potted ficus, Brette wrinkled her nose. "God spare us," she muttered to the leaf she fingered.

She seemed edgy tonight, less confident and gregarious than he'd ever observed her. Did she fear someone would be crass enough to mention her questionable birth? Or did she worry she'd be called upon to sing? Perhaps she'd experienced the elder Miss Gambwell's vocal talents before and didn't relish a repeat performance?

"What was that, Miss Culpepper? Can't you sing?" Miss Gambwell's shrewd gaze and sly smile suggested she already knew the answer. Today the she-cat deemed Brette worthy to speak to when in Hyde Park she'd acted as if Brette were beneath her touch?

The Gambwells fell far short of Brette in his

estimation. All women did.

"Certainly, I *can* sing. I do possess vocal cords, after all. But so do cows, cats, and crocodiles. Because someone *can* do something doesn't mean they should."

Touché, ma petite.

Alex chuckled and raised his glass in silent salute. His Brette had pluck. He'd give her that.

She grinned in return, but her smile faded quickly when Phillip Lapley slithered near. "I hoped I might have the privilege of hearing you perform, Miss Culpepper."

Why so attentive now?

Had he learned of her change in circumstances? His kind sniffed out new heiresses with the finesse and accuracy of well-trained bloodhounds.

"Trust me, Mr. Lapley, you wouldn't say so afterward. I hopelessly lack talent." She peered beyond him and stopped tormenting the bush. "Lady Covington isn't in attendance with you this evening?"

"Er ... alas no." He gave her what he probably believed a charming smile. Looked more like a grinning porpoise.

Unfair to the porpoise.

Shoulders slumped and eyes cast down, Lapley affected a sorrowful mien. "I'm saddened to say, Lady Covington has set aside her affection for me."

Probably caught him in a compromising position. For the umpteenth time.

Why would the Goodinghams have invited such a vulgar character to dine? Were they truly that desperate to even their dinner number? Lapley might've been the grandson of a viscount, but his reputation as a womanizing rake didn't make him appropriate company for innocents like their cow-eyed daughter.

The timid mouse fidgeting with her fan couldn't have been more than sixteen. Had they taken leave of their senses?

"I believe after-dinner entertainment includes dancing." And if it didn't, Alex had deliberately dropped a robust hint in his hosts' ears. Since he and Raven outranked the other guests, they'd be obliged to accommodate him. Bold as brass of him, and beyond the pale. He'd possibly put his hostess in a quandary, but she'd oblige.

Particularly since her daughter was of marriageable age, though barely, and he was available. An earl but a few short weeks and already a string of eligible misses had been paraded before him. God help him when the Marriage Mart was once again in full swing, and he took his obligatory seat in the House of Lords.

Beggars eyed a crust of bread with less longing than the bevy of lustful glances he'd received of late.

"Right you are, Wycombe," Mr. Goodingham boomed. "My daughter's eager to practice her steps and her playing. I've paid her music and dance instructors a fortune."

Goodingham's investments in India cotton and silk filled his pockets to bursting. A fat purse opened many doors otherwise closed to men of his ilk. If Brette possessed a grand inheritance, her birth mightn't be of importance to the *ton* either.

Alex positively didn't give a fig which side of the blanket she'd been born on. However, he'd certainly like to share a bed with her, and discover if the rest of her skin was anywhere near as creamy as the tempting mounds mere inches away.

Another notion he wouldn't have dared a few weeks ago, and he aimed a glance ceilingward. Swifter than a rock tossed in the ocean's depths, he'd descended into carnal sinfulness.

Would the Almighty smite him? *For putting off false piety*? For having thoughts he didn't act upon? He couldn't help but think God favored an honest heart above outward pretense.

At least Alex would live and die a happier man.

Goodingham beamed with fatherly pride and affection as he brushed his side whiskers. "Millie floats like an angel upon the dance floor, if I do say so myself."

"Float?" Margaret Gambwell whispered to Alex. "Not hardly with those dimply feet and chubby thighs" After her spiteful remark, she drifted away, and Lapley skittered after her, making straight for Miss Millie Goodingham.

His next unfortunate victim? Hopefully, her parents grew wise to his guiles.

At last, the tardy guests arrived, and moments later, the dinner gong pealed. Everyone swung their attention to their American hostess.

"Please, we won't stand on formality tonight. We've enough of politesse when the Season is full on, don't we?" Mrs. Goodingham tittered and fluttered her fingertips. "Do find yourself a partner to walk through with."

"Well," huffed Lady Gambwell, caustic disapproval drawing the word out. "How ... provincial. I suppose one should expect bumpkin behavior from a colonial." Her lip curling the merest bit, her superior gaze veered to Brette. "And others as ill-bred."

Brette flipped open her fan, mischief twinkling in her eyes. A man could lose himself in those glimmering pools of green-ringed blue. She fanned herself lightly. "Ah, indeed. Especially those hiding their lack of breeding and refinement beneath pretty outward trappings and pretentiousness." Lips tilted, she blinked innocently, as she nonchalantly fluttered her lace-edged fan. "Don't you agree, your ladyship?"

Alex hadn't witnessed a viper bite, but given Lady Gambwell's slit eyes and bared teeth, a lethal attack loomed. Instead, she presented her ramrod stiff spine and all but stomped away.

He cupped Brette's shoulder, whispering, "Please let me take you through. I refuse to escort one of those Gambwell terrors."

"All right. Should we warn her parents, do you think?" Brette jutted her chin toward Lapley fawning over the blushing Miss Goodingham's hand.

Even before Brette had finished her sentence, Mrs. Goodingham rescued the violated appendage and tucked her daughter's palm neatly into the crook of her arm. After offering a cordial, if forced, smile, she murmured a few words to Lapley and towed her smitten daughter away.

"No, her mother's well aware he's a fortune hunter." Alex cupped Brette's elbow as he rotated them toward the dining room. He deliberately held back, waiting for the others to precede them. "I beg you, please save me a dance after supper. If, that is, you can forgive me for my idiocy yesterday."

A waltz. A legitimate excuse to hold her in his arms. More fool he for willingly enduring the torture.

He hadn't danced with her since her first foray into the Social World, a few months ago.

A waste of time this, persisting in a fantasy doomed to an unhappy ending. Pure foolishness.

Yet he must ask her.

Brette's incredible eyes filled with gentleness. "I was about to ask you the same thing. I regret hurting you, Alex, but my situation is... Well, you know my circumstances. You must be wise and not act impulsively. A union between us would not serve you at all well."

He lifted a shoulder. "There's nothing to forgive. I must beg your pardon for putting you in an awkward position. We've not ever discussed a match between us, but I shan't regret asking you."

Hand on Raven's arm, Lady Ravensdale glanced behind her as she exited. Her expression clearly said, *Stop chatting and come along.*

"My sister bids us, but I should be delighted to save you a set. I adore dancing, and you're keen on your feet." A glint lit Brette's eyes. "Almost as keen as I am."

Alex arched a brow wickedly. "Ah, we shall see. I don't suppose you'd care to wager on that? "

"And how would we determine the winner of such a bet?" Brette's swift retort bordered on flirtatious.

Hmm, perhaps he should consider a third proposal

and do it right this time. Flowers, a few poetic phrases, on one knee. All that sort of thing. And a ring, of course. Something unusual, but enchanting, exactly like her. Perhaps a turquoise tourmaline or an aquamarine.

Don't get ahead of yourself, old chap. Half an hour ago, you'd sworn off ever considering making another offer. Because she smiles and flirts doesn't mean she'll say yes. Bide your time. Determine which way the wind blows before making an utter arse of yourself again.

What seemed like endless boring hours later, the men having finished their port and cigars, and the women their after-dinner tea, everyone reassembled in the parlor. Even with the furniture pushed to the perimeters, only three or four couples could take to the floor at one time.

As for privacy? None, whatsoever.

Unless he maneuvered his partner to the terrace beyond the slightly parted French windows. Given the crisp chill that had crept into his overcoat and beneath his top hat during the carriage ride, Brette wouldn't welcome a stroll outdoors, more was the pity.

Brette excused herself, and the Gambwell misses followed suit

Pleading urgency caused by her delicate condition, Brooke promptly set out after her sister

... cousin.

And when Lady Gambwell also slipped from the room, like a snake after an unsuspecting rabbit, Raven shook his head. "Do you think we'll need to send in reinforcements?"

A lively discourse would no doubt take place. Alex would've liked to be an insect in the retiring room when it did.

"You leave it to me," volunteered Mrs. Goodingham. "I'll not have those uppity harpies harassing my guests." She leaned in and whispered conspiratorially, her American twang both endearing and annoying. "They're here tonight because Millie fancies Harriet Gambwell her dearest friend. And you'll notice, the chit didn't bother to come."

"Perhaps she's indisposed." Alex doubted it.

"No. She was invited to the Fosters' ducal residence for the weekend, *after* her mother accepted our invitation." With that starchy disclosure, she marched from the overwarm room.

Alex took a position near the terrace doors, welcoming the cold air, as much to cool his ardor as his person. He'd been in a constant state of arousal since encountering Brette outside her solicitor's office and a series of cold baths kept him—*it*—subdued. It seemed when he'd cast off his clerical strappings, all the worldliness he'd managed to hold at bay had crashed into him in one huge wave.

More likely, his carnal inclinations had lain dormant until he met Brette, and now, much like his playful pup, they cavorted about, unrestrained. Netting the wind was easier than subduing them. And yet he must resist temptation, no matter how enchanting he found her. He'd not risk a two-decade-old friendship for another delicious kiss, for next time Raven would surely call him out. Or demand Brette marry him.

And Alex wouldn't have her forced into a union she obviously objected to.

The women returned en masse, none appearing the worse for wear, though a decidedly strained smile arched Lady Gambwell's lips and a storm brewed in Lady Ravensdale's eyes.

At her mother's urging, and most reluctantly from the petulant pout she sported, Miss Goodingham settled onto the needlepoint-covered stool before the harpsichord. She gazed longingly at Mr. Lapley, but after her mother's firmly whispered admonition in her ear, Miss Goodingham complied, opening the sheet music. Sulking, she played the waltz's opening stanzas.

Alex promptly found his way to Brette's side and angled his back to the others, intent on claiming a dance. He'd seize every opportunity to hold her in his arms. "May I be so bold as to request this dance? I noticed

Lapley eyeing you. I'd spare you that trial. He can't boast the agility of a whale, and he'll mash your toes."

Brette darted Lapley a reserved glance. "I would enjoy a dance, but I must tell you, after what occurred in the retiring room, I expect Brooke to plead a headache and depart soon."

After an indecipherable glance toward Lady Ravensdale, Brette accepted his arm, and he swung her dainty form into his embrace.

A perfect fit.

Like a custom-made glove, his right palm cradled her ribs, his other a faultless nest for her delicate hand. He rubbed his thumb over her rib, noting, with no small amount of manly pride, her sudden intake of breath. Bending his neck the merest bit, he inhaled her intoxicating perfume. Wherever they touched or brushed together with the dance's flowing movement, awareness, powerful and invigorating, sprang to life.

Sweet torture he never wanted to end.

For an instant, he lost track of where he was, until the crowded impromptu dance floor caused him to nearly twirl Brette into another couple. To prevent the collision, Alex drew her scandalously close, their torsos bumping from chest to hip.

Molten desire engulfed him.

His mouth went dry as parchment, his tongue

sticking to the roof. *God, think of something else.* He swallowed. "What happened to upset Brooke?"

"Lady Gambwell gleefully informed us your grandmother is so set against me and a possible union between us, that she'll stop at nothing to ruin me. Including fabricating and spreading tales to *le beau monde.*" Brette glanced up, amusement wrestling with disquiet in her gaze. She wasn't as unaffected as she pretended.

Grandmother could expect a terse visit on the morrow. He'd bloody damned well tolerated enough of people dictating to him and trying to control his life. "Tales? What sort of tales?"

Brette's gaze sought his for an instant before flitting away. "She claims my mother was a prostitute."

The bumpy road to hell is paved with
good intentions corrupted by prejudices,
misunderstandings, ignorance, and fears.
*~Appearances and Attitude—The Genteel Lady's
Guide to Practical Living*

10

Shouldn't Brette be more outraged and disgusted by the Dowager Countess Wycombe? Gloating Lady Gambwell? And her positively vile daughters? Perhaps if she cared a whit what they thought, she might've been, but as Mother had sagely advised, only the opinions of those you love mattered.

Toss the others in the rubbish bin.

Except for going rigid as a poker, Alex hadn't responded to her crude revelation.

Brette peeked at him, mindful not to seem overly interested. She wanted to stare boldly, but with so many eyes watching, daren't.

She hadn't meant to burden him with the tattle, but as much as she tried to ignore the nastiness and pretend she didn't give a fig what those venom-tongued harpies believed, their malice bruised a mite.

His regard sank to hers, and the outrage simmering in his eyes did her heart good. "A vicious lie, I'll vow."

He wouldn't believe the scurrilous accusation, even if she couldn't be as certain. If Mr. Shipwreck could locate a marriage record, or if someone who'd known her mother would come forward. But why would they after all this time?

"I cannot be absolutely positive Lady Gambwell's prattle is fictitious, though I fervently hope she's mistaken." Bastardry was horrid enough, but the offspring of a strumpet too? How could anyone disregard so shameful a yoke?

Alex made a gruff, sympathetic noise in his throat, pressing his strong hand lightly into her side, and a shiver of desire danced across her shoulders, rippled down her spine, and came to rest heavily in her hips.

"How distressing this must be for you, Brette."

Others bullying me because of my birth? Or you holding me wonderfully close, yet I know I'm unsuitable for your regard?

She gave herself a mental shake. *Don't be a nincompoop.* He referred to the condemnation, of course.

Earnestness tightened the planes of his face. "I wish I could do something other than tell my grandmother to stubble it and retract her claws where you're concerned.

You will tell me if there's anything, won't you?"

Sincerely wish to marry her.

Stop your foolishness. He cannot.

Twice he'd spontaneously—*half-heartedly*—proposed. Was he opposed to genuine, affectionate declarations?

Certainly her station made it impossible to accept him, but a part of her, the romantic who adored bringing other couples together, wanted a fairytale proposal. A declaration of love. Not merely a by-the-by, if you haven't anything else to do with your life, I suppose we might marry.

Or had pity motivated Alex and prompted his asking? He'd shown his compassionate, sacrificing nature many times, so the notion wasn't altogether impossible.

Wholly humiliating, however.

"I presume your solicitor has everything well in hand?" He glanced downward for a moment, kindness and something warmer evident in his eyes.

Brette nodded once and edged nearer. "He's trying to discover whether my parents ever married. I can better plan for my future once I know one way or the other."

Opening an establishment wasn't as far-fetched an idea as it had been a week ago. A respectable woman didn't dare, but a by-blow might. Especially since she possessed her own funds now. But would patrons frequent such a shoppe if owned by someone of questionable pedigree?

"It matters naught to me, and I sincerely apologize on my grandmother's behalf. I shall speak with her tomorrow. She'll cease her futile quest, or, so help me God, I'll cut her funding off." He skillfully steered them away from the Gambwells, lined up like discontented, ready-to-pounce watchdogs beside the hearth.

Brette kept perfect time with him, anticipating his steps, unlike her partners she'd had before. She and Alex danced as one, their movements perfectly coordinated, their souls united for this brief time.

Fanciful imagining on her part, but wonderfully so.

"Oddly enough, Alex, I rather admire her determination to protect you and the title." And Brette did. Everyone ought to have a loyal champion. "Not the dowager's methods, of course, but her caring passionately for you and your future."

Alex's short, harsh laugh drew several curious glances, and the anger in his eyes deepened them to hunter green, the silvery specks in his irises glinting bright against the deeper hue. "Trust me, her interference has nothing to do with great affection for me, and everything to do with the earldom and *her* position. She'd sacrifice her own child if she believed it would improve her social standing one jot."

He spun her in a slow circle, and, to raise the Gambwell chits' hackles, Brette graced him with her most winsome smile.

A slow grin creased his face.

Sliding the merest bit closer, she whispered, "I know it's indecorous, and I should eschew childish behavior, but I do enjoy making the Gambwells jealous. I believe Charlotte's gnashing her teeth." Brette darted a swift glance her nemesis's way. "Yes, yes, she is. And Margaret looks like she's considering hurling that shepherdess figurine at my head."

Alex leveled the chit a direct, don't-you-dare look, and she jerked her hostile attention away, pointedly studying the fireplace's hand-painted tiles.

This time, his melodious chuckle made them the target of several inquisitive looks. He canted his head at the Gambwells. "Let's give them something to be jealous of, shall we? Nothing too unseemly, but enough to stick in their craws for a day or two. If you're up to it."

Was he challenging her?

She examined his face, and only warm regard registered there. But yes, deep within his eyes, a spark of rebellion glowed. Amazing he'd managed to keep this part of his nature subdued as Reverend Hawksworth.

No doubt an answering glint reflected in her eyes,

for as much as she adored the hubbub and commotion of the *haut ton*, their loftier airs rankled. As long as she didn't engage in anything too scandalous. She couldn't resist. "What did you have in mind?"

He expertly steered her toward the French doors. "A stroll along the terrace should suffice. It'll be cold."

Probably freezing.

"Well, as I'm quite warm—" Roasting. Her dampened underarms testified to that truth.

Though whether the dancing in the hot parlor or her sensual awareness of him should be blamed, she couldn't determine. "I'd be grateful for a few moments of refreshing air."

And the Gambwells *would* have a conniption fit. A reddened nose and chicken-skin arms were worth it. A ghost of a smile tickled her mouth. My, she'd become something of a rebel.

Across the room, she met Brooke's questioning gaze, and mouthed, "Outside."

Brooke gave a brief nod then directed her attention to the mantel clock before subtly raising her hand, fingers splayed. Five minutes. And Brooke would watch the time. They'd no doubt leave afterward.

In one fluid motion, Alex released Brette's hand and toed the door open so he could exit before her. He deftly swept her through the opening and onto the terrace.

The frigid air hit her with a bone-chilling blast, and she sucked in a small, startled gasp. It was positively freezing. Silvery frost iced the grass and shrubberies already. However, the stars, bright in the ebony sky, twinkled and winked cheerfully, and the half-moon lazily hanging on the horizon appeared to blink as a wispy cloud drifted by.

She leaned her hips against the balustrade and rubbed her arms. "*Brrr.*" Alex stepped beside her, mere inches shy of touching her.

Brette longed to lean into his sturdy heat, enjoy his arms about her as he held her close and warmed her. She yearned to run her fingers through his curls and discover their texture. Most of all, she wanted him to gaze at her with the same unreserved adoration Heath and Tristan looked at their wives.

Silly, selfish dreams, but if one didn't dream, didn't have hope, have something to anticipate and look forward to, what was left?

Work? Drudgery? Despair?

Hope deferred makes the heart sick.

Alex had preached on the topic the last time she'd attended his church. Yes, better to cling to optimism, no matter how slight.

She shivered and clenched her teeth to hush their chattering. Her exposed flesh raised, nubby and rough. Chicken skin? More like a plucked goose.

Alex shifted closer until they touched from calf to shoulder. Utterly glorious, and perhaps a mite *risqué*.

She sneaked a peek into the parlor behind her. As she'd expected.

Brooke, chatting with Mr. Goodingham, stood guard near the French window. Beyond them Margaret, Charlotte, and Miss Goodingham danced. Mrs. Goodingham must have taken to playing.

"Have you news from your alibis?" Brette didn't doubt he'd eventually clear his name, but in the interim, the mud-slinging could be damaging.

Alex glanced down, slanting his mouth into a slight smile. "Yes, and they've corroborated my story. Whoever suggested that I may have been involved in the tragedy will have to go elsewhere to stir their mischief."

Arms crossed, she hunched into herself, wishing she could burrow into his embrace. "Do you have a notion who might have done so?"

He shook his head, the moonlight glinting off the top. "Not for certain, but it could've been a number of distant relatives hoping to inherit if I hanged. Of greater concern to me is whether the fire was an accident. Once the footman is located, I'm sure we'll have the whole of it."

Alex stated it casually, without rancor, as if it were the most natural thing in the world to have people want him dead. He possessed a far more forgiving nature than she.

"I understood that the footman was questioned already." Lord, but the cold numbed her toes.

Yet this time with Alex was too precious to forego. Oh, all right, and the longer they lingered outdoors, the more peeved the Gambwells grew.

He grazed his jaw with his fingertips and gave an affirmative nod. "I believe he was. The maid too. But when the accusation arose against me, the footman disappeared. Slightly suspicious, I'd say, and it sickens me to think someone intended to kill my cousin and his son. Lawrence was only thirteen, poor chap."

"Yes, it's utterly dreadful." She clasped his forearm, fear for him congealing her blood. "Alex, do be careful. People are wont to take desperate measures for power and position, and it seems to me, someone means you harm."

He laid his warm palm on her arm, and she wanted to melt into his body's heat. "Don't distress yourself. I've taken precautions, and I've hired Bow Street runners to look into finding the wayward servant and to determine the fire's cause. Can't help to have my own people investigating as well, I should think."

Someone evil enough to try to convince the authorities he was guilty of murdering his cousins. A malicious person wouldn't stop after one attempt. He must know that too, yet he appeared composed.

Should something happen to him— She hugged her shoulders as a fear induced shudder shook her. *Stop*. She refused to contemplate the horror.

Alex tucked her a mite closer to his side—close enough, in fact, that she smelled his cologne.

So manly, yet clean. Not heavy or cloying.

"I'd offer you my coat, but I fear I cannot put it on again without assistance. I've been imposing on footmen until I hire a valet." He chuckled and bunched his shoulders to demonstrate. "See, the dashed thing allows me little room for movement. The fashion might be all the crack, but I've wondered the entire week what I'll do if I have to move suddenly. Perhaps rescue a damsel in distress or stop a runaway steed. I fear the seams will rip completely apart."

"I rather like how it looks on you."

Assessing him from the corner of her eye, Brette fingered her lovely gown's overskirt. His coat hugged his shoulders and chest and outlined his arm muscles nicely. His simple cleric clothing, though serviceable and clean, hadn't been tailored and hid his impressive physique.

Hand to his chest, Alex bent into a shallow bow, his proximity to her and the balustrade preventing anything more gallant. "Then for you, I shall make the sacrifice."

She shivered again.

"You're cold. Let's return to the drawing room."

He took her elbow, and as one, they faced the door as Brooke stepped outside.

"Brette, we're leaving now." Brooke's smile turned radiant when Heath joined her and tucked her into his side. "You'll both catch your death out here. Come away at once."

Alex placed his hand on Brette's arm. "Ride with me tomorrow, before breaking our fast."

She searched his face, the surprisingly dark eyebrows, high cheekbones, and strong, squarish jaw. The lips he'd pressed to hers once. And his mesmerizing eyes, the moonlight reflecting in their depths. Alex's gaze sank to her mouth, and she bit the inside of her cheek to keep from running her tongue over her lower lip.

Not wise. Not wise at all. Say no.

Her traitorous tongue refused to obey logic. "All right." She'd allow herself one more memory.

"At half past—"

"Heath?" Brooke clutched her belly, panic and pain riddling her voice.

Coatless, his cravat tossed across the sofa's back, Alex nursed a brandy before the library's dying fire. The gilt bronze mantle clock chimed the quarter hour.

Nearly two.

Tomorrow, he'd pay for the late hour with gritty eyes and a wooly head, but at present, he was too damned comfortable to move. Not even anticipation of his and Brette's early morning jaunt to Hyde Park stirred him.

She'd call it off, in any event, so why seek his mattress's comfort?

Shoeless, his legs stretched before him and his ankles crossed, he rested his head against the chair's high back. Shutting his eyes, he released a long, rumbling sigh. He'd never prayed as fervently, pleading and petitioning the Almighty to spare Raven and Brooke's child, as he had this night.

Shifting, Alex grimaced and rubbed his leg.

It ached from kneeling before the chair he now sat in, but he'd do so again in a blink.

Brooke must stay abed for a spell to recover from a vicious bout of food poisoning, not premature labor after all. The babe would bear no long-lasting ill effects.

Thank God.

How had Brette fared through the ordeal?

He hadn't seen her since the coach had skidded to a stop in front of the house. Before a footman opened the vehicle's door, she'd pressed the latch, jumped to the ground, and calmly and firmly began issuing orders.

From the first instant she'd detected Brooke's distress, Brette had taken the situation in hand, and with a general's boldness and efficiency too. She'd told Lady Gambwell to stubble it and move her rotund self aside as Brette cleared the way for Heath, carrying Brooke, to rush past and out into the night.

And God forgive Alex, he'd chuckled at the offended expression on the woman's face as he'd passed and saluted her.

Utterly priceless.

Unwise to underestimate his petite spitfire. Yes, indeed.

Grinning in remembrance, Alex sipped the superb brandy and exhaled a long breath again. Raven kept the finest spirits on hand, and tonight, Alex had indulged in two—or was it three?—full tumblers' worth; something he rarely did.

He ought to drag his sore self to bed, but the liquor and snug fire had succeeded in lulling him into a drowsy, half-conscious state, and it took rather too much effort to stir himself to the point of rising.

Should he look in on Domino before he retired? Not this late.

Alex needed a few hours rest without the playful terror frolicking about in his bed, nibbling toes, fingers, and ears with needle-sharp teeth, and besides, Cook had fallen in love with the rascally pup and had made him a nice box in the larder.

Not bothering to cover his mouth, Alex yawned widely. The room tilted and slowly spun 'round and 'round

Blast me. Might be half-foxed.

He chuckled and took another swig. He hadn't been soused since learning his uncle had abandoned his parish and run off with a nun, leaving Alex to step in as the new rector.

The fire gave a pair of valiant, yet weak, crackles, even as the coals faded more. Shortly, darkness would claim the already cooling chamber. No help for it. He'd have to drag his tipsy self upstairs.

He reluctantly cracked an eye open.

Or the couch would suffice for the night, but the single crocheted throw wouldn't provide much warmth. However, it might be worth the discomfort to send the unflappable Jenkin into a dither upon discovering Alex snoring away tomorrow—ah, this morning.

The study door whooshed open, and Brette glided in, her cloud of fairy pale hair floating around her shoulders and back, the ends teasing her rounded buttocks. Wearing a pale green robe and matching slippers, she pushed her hair behind one shoulder as she hurried to a bookshelf.

What was she about this time of the morning?

Holding the candle high, she scoured the volumes, her mouth moving silently as she read the titles, touching their spines with her forefinger.

"Aha." She made a satisfied sound in the back of her throat and bent to examine a rather formidable-looking book on a lower shelf.

Alex inhaled sharply, his breath suspended as the outline of her perfectly formed bottom, tipped upward at a most delicious and provocative angle. A gentleman would've averted his attention. He would've mere weeks ago, but tonight, he made no effort to do so, but instead slanted his head for a slightly better view.

I've become a complete lecher.

Brette gasped and straightened, swinging to face the chairs. "Who's there?"

Devil it. He'd frightened her and would have to reveal himself.

He bent forward, allowing her to see him clearly, and wiggled the fingers of his free hand. "I am. Didn't mean to alarm you." Excellent. He didn't sound as foxed as his spinning head suggested. He waved at the hefty book she held. "That looks impossibly droll. Having trouble sleeping and came in search of the most boring tome the library boasts?"

She visibly relaxed and summoned a forgiving smile. "No, I thought to dabble in a little reading about business and enterprise."

Why? Alex examined the ominous book again. "Most assuredly you'll be asleep within minutes of cracking it open if that's truly what you've selected."

Three fine rows creased her forehead, and she glanced at the book. She set the volume and the candle aside before crossing to him. Her gown floated about her hips and legs, swishing softly with her movements, and her hair swayed, silky curls entwining about her shoulders and arms.

"A nymph," he muttered, before taking another

swallow, savoring the mellow heat trickling to his belly.

"A nymph, am I?" She arched a fine eyebrow as she bent over him, slouched in his chair.

She sniffed, her adorable nose crinkling. "Alex? Have you been drinking?"

Nodding and grinning like an imbecile, he raised his glass. "I prayed first though."

He couldn't tear his attention from the luscious display inches from his eyes. Her gown gaped enough to give him a glimpse of the creamy globes within, and his groin reacted predictably.

Impure imaginings clanged around in his head. Hell, he wasn't a saint. Far from it, truth to tell. But this was his Brette, his sweet, innocent Brette, and he wouldn't ogle her like a drunken sailor. He dragged his reluctant focus upward to her soft mouth and higher yet to her sympathetic eyes.

Instead of harping or scolding, she brushed his hair from his forehead with her cook fingertips. "I was utterly terrified for Brooke and the baby. I confess, I'm still tense. I suppose it will take a while to recover." She caught her lip between her teeth, and eyed his glass. "Might I have a taste?"

Silently, Alex extended the tumbler.

Giving him a half-smile, she tossed off the last speck of amber liquid and promptly coughed and gasped. "Good heavens," she managed between wheezes. "You might've warned me. It's burning clear to my belly."

His regard locked on her hands pressed to her middle, flattening the planes of her gown tight against her stomach and sloping hips.

Her expression dreamy, she closed her eyes. "It feels rather nice, sort of like when you wake from a nap. Cozy and warm and drowsy."

Opening her sultry eyes, Brette's lips slowly bent upward. An innocent, she couldn't know the siren's invitation in her gaze or that, with her flushed cheeks, half-closed lids, and parted lips, she resembled a woman thoroughly made love to.

Blister it.

Alex dragged her onto his lap, and except for inhaling a brief, startled breath, she appeared unperturbed by his action. He buried his face in her neck, relishing the dove-soft skin, her sweet, clean fragrance, and the weight of her rounded bottom on his lap.

Desire—immediate, electric, and consuming—shot through him.

You're in deep trouble, old chap. Stop this nonsense before you regret it.

If Brette had objected, pulled away, or voiced her

displeasure, he might have been able to heed his conscience's chiding. Instead, she sagged into him, draping one slender arm around his neck, and splayed her other hand against his chest as she angled her neck, allowing him greater access.

He trailed fiery kisses along the ivory length, lingering at the sensitive spot behind her ear. A half-moan, half-sigh whispered from her when he licked the tender flesh. Smiling, he dotted her face and jaw with more heated kisses before working his way to her slack mouth.

Scarcely an inch between their lips, Alex waited. He'd give her the choice, let her decide to continue or not.

Brette cupped his face with both hands and brought his mouth to hers, moving the plump pillows across his as he'd taught her the first time. She tentatively searched his mouth with her tongue, her exploration becoming bolder as her hunger grew She tasted of brandy and tea and a trifle minty too.

Desire exploded, shattering the last remnants of his self-control. He'd loathe himself afterward, but right now, nothing mattered but Brette. He wanted to tell her he loved her, adored her, but her earlier rejections made him leery. Afraid she'd flee, he kept silent, instead worshipping her with his mouth and hands.

"Alex,' she moaned, arching into him.

A groan started low in his belly and worked its way to his throat. Alex shifted Brette, laying her across his knees, an arm cradling her back. With his free hand, he explored the loveliness her gown shielded.

The enchantress in his lap tangled her tongue with his, as if she too couldn't control the fiery desire urging her onward. On the verge of completely losing control, he cupped her derrière, kneading the firm flesh, and suckled her lower lip.

His penis, hot, heavy, and demanding, pulsed beneath her thigh.

What are you doing?

Brette wasn't a lightskirt or fast chit. She was the ward of one of his dearest friends. The woman Alex loved. His morals chafed stridently at his behavior, at taking advantage of her inexperience and attraction to him, and the spirits he'd consumed couldn't be blamed either.

He wanted her. Plain and simple. But as his wife, not a frenzied tupping when drink dulled his senses and the day's events caused both of their emotions to run high.

Gently pulling away, he captured her exploring hands, and rested his forehead against hers. "Brette, love, we must stop."

She gave a shaky nod, her lips glowing rosy from his kisses. "I know."

No insurmountable obstacles prevented them from marrying. Her background mattered naught, his grandmother's and family's acceptance of her even less. And as for the *ton*'s approval...? Indeed, perhaps the time had come to drop well-placed hints about those without sin casting stones.

Numerous lofty peers and peeresses would tumble from their self-appointed pedestals if their indiscretions became public. He wouldn't stoop to blackmail, but a preventive whisper here and there couldn't go amiss if it protected Brette from their hypocritical censure.

No, nothing major hindered their joining, except Charlbury's fire. Until he knew the cause, he wouldn't risk Brette's safety. They had plenty of time, in any event. After all, mourning restricted his marrying any time soon, but he could still court her.

Fully aware of how his dazzling looks affected women, he refused to play the carefree charmer for Brette. Their relationship must be built on sincerity and trust. A woman of her character didn't kiss a man, didn't respond as she had unless her emotions were engaged. Of that, he hadn't a single doubt.

"I ... I don't know what came over me." She blushed, an adorable rosy pink tinging her cheeks.

He did, for the same firestorm consumed him, and the knowledge made him more determined to make her his.

Biting her lip, her color still high, Brette modestly pushed her robe lower. For someone short of stature, she possessed the most exquisite legs. Long, elegant thighs—the skin pearly white—that curved into graceful calves before tapering into the daintiest of ankles.

He clenched his jaw to stubble the involuntary protest springing to his tongue as the gauzy fabric covered the tempting lengths.

"Here, let's sit you up." He helped her to an upright position, gritting his teeth when her rounded bottom pressed into his rigid groin. "I must beg your pardon and forgiveness."

"Why?" Brette swept her hair over one shoulder then twisted the glorious flaxen tendrils into a thick rope. The end curled around her breast, the nipple pressing pebble-hard against her robe's delicate fabric.

He swallowed and directed his gaze to the two or three remaining coals glowing in the hearth. "I shouldn't have kissed you. You're overwrought, and I took advantage."

"I kissed you first, and if anyone took advantage, it was me." She pointed at the empty tumbler on the side table, her slightly swollen mouth bending into a winning smile. "I shan't insult either of us by pretending I didn't thoroughly enjoy it."

No feminine qualms, no pretense at affront, Brette's directness was equally refreshing and disconcerting.

"You seemed practiced at the art." She scooted off his lap, her gown settling around her trim ankles.

Alex nearly choked on his surprise.

Good God, was she asking how experienced he was?

She'd be surprised to learn, not so much. Once or twice at university when the other young bucks had sown their oats.

He possessed neither the temperament nor coin to indulge in pleasures of the flesh, and the whole concept of paying women for sexual favors rather disgusted him. Those unfortunates were also someone's daughters. And casual trysts, simply to enjoy a woman's soft curves for an hour or two, hadn't appealed.

"A gentleman doesn't discuss matters of that nature." Curving his mouth, he too rose.

She cocked her head. "Even with a woman he's proposed to twice?"

The muted light made it impossible to read her face, but surely her voice held a wistful note, and his hope burgeoned.

"Especially to such a woman." He winked, rakishly. "He wouldn't want her opinion of him to diminish."

"It couldn't." She gathered her book and candlestick, shyness and yearning playing upon her features. "Shall we walk up together?"

Definitely an invitation. One he was honor-bound to refuse.

"Not yet. I need to look in on Domino." Bloody poor excuse, but he seized it.

He helped himself to the two-pronged candelabra on Raven's desk then used an ember to

light one taper. Raven wouldn't mind, and Alex would return the stand first thing in the morning. He couldn't stumble to the kitchen or his room in the dark, could he?

Brette continued to stand there, hesitant and uncertain, as if striving to summon the nerve to say something. He feared he knew what she wanted to ask, and his answer must be no. Time to distract her and send her on her way.

"I presume our outing to Hyde Park must be postponed?"

She dipped her head. "Yes, but—"

"Just as well," he rushed on, arranging the fire

screen snug against the tiles. She mustn't voice what he suspected she wanted to ask. He mightn't have the strength to refuse, and he'd hate himself afterward. If and when he bedded her, it would be honorably, as his wife. Not a rushed dalliance with her sister and brother-in-law but a few doors away.

"I wish—"

"I'll likely not rouse before noon. I indulged too freely, I'm afraid." He forced a chuckle, the sound insincere even to his ears.

"Alex?"

He sighed, and she wrinkled her forehead, obviously confused.

How could she not be? He'd sent her mixed signals, and in her inexperience, she couldn't understand that his eagerness to have her gone had nothing to do with her and everything to do with his tenuous grip on his self-control.

No help for it. He'd have to force her to go.

He covered the distance between them and, after kissing her forehead, turned her toward the door and gave a little shove. "Go to bed, Brette. You cannot be found here, with me, this time of night. Your reputation is already perilously fragile."

"Yes, of course. You're right. Goodnight, Alex." She gave him a final, probing look.

What did she seek? Apparently, she didn't find whatever it was. Shoulders slumping and appearing utterly lost, she glided from the study as silently as she'd arrived.

"Won't be tempted more than you can endure?" he muttered after she'd gone. "Honestly, Lord. That wasn't more than I could endure?" Because he'd nearly reached the point of no resistance, and he didn't much like himself at the moment. The part of him still aching for release gave an angry twitch.

Yes, but if you take her to bed, she'd have to wed you.

Was the notion so horrid?

Not for him, but Brette must come to the match willingly. Because she wanted it—wanted him—as much as he wanted her. Any other start to their marriage would be perpetual sand in their sheets, a constant niggling reminder.

After collecting his things, he waited five minutes before following Brette. Plenty of time for her to make her way upstairs. He quickly peeked in on Domino. As expected, the pup lay sound asleep, nose tucked beneath his spotted tail upon a distinctly unmanly lavender ruffled pillow, a bone nearly as big as the pup's leg beside him.

Alex sniffed then sniffed again. Roses? An

eyebrow shot skyward.

Cook had bathed the dog in rose water?

Poor chap; his dignity would be sorely frayed if he knew.

Tiptoeing from the kitchen, Alex headed to the stairway. The smell of an extinguished candle wafted past, and he turned in a slow, cautious circle, seeking the source. There, in the drawing room, tucked onto the bay window seat, her arms folded around her knees and her face buried in them, huddled Brette.

Weeping.

12

Indulging in a second cup of chocolate, liberally topped with Devonshire cream, Brette rested her head against the windowpane.

Snoring lightly, Freddy lay curled at her feet, a gray-spattered forepaw covering his equally silvery nose. He was getting old, though he'd perked up a bit with Domino to keep him company.

Outside, everything glistened from the sun's rays reflecting upon the icy crystals clinging to most surfaces. A frosty lace-like pattern edged several windows, a testament to the mid-morning's frigid temperature. Coldness radiated through the beveled glass; a startling contrast to the warm cup she held.

Rather like her fickle emotions, first cold then hot

then cold again.

Bah. She'd become a feckless, indecisive beef-wit.

A few brave souls garbed in thick layers of warm clothing dotted the sidewalk and streets, and a horseman, his multi-colored knitted scarf covering his lower face to guard against the nippiness, leisurely ambled past the house. He boldly stared in the ground floor windows and brazenly touched his hat's rim when he spied Brette tucked snuggly in the bay window.

His cheekiness earned him a tiny, closed-mouth smile, but no wave in return. Definitely outside the bounds, that. The horse's single white fetlock jarred her memory. She'd seen the gelding before. Probably in Hyde Park on one of her many walks or rides.

Less than eight hours ago, she'd sat in this same spot, softly weeping, afraid she'd be overheard in her chamber. She waited behind the drawing room's open door until Alex had left the study before seeking the cozy refuge and giving vent to her tears.

When they'd kissed last night, she'd come face-to-face with the undeniable truth. Finally admitted what she suspected, what her heart knew and had hinted at for months.

She loved him. Irrevocably and desperately.

Last night, she'd tried to tell him, and also explain her wanton behavior.

Though the words hadn't come easily—embarrassment had thickened her tongue—she'd wanted him to know she wouldn't have behaved brazenly unless she loved him. She couldn't give him her body without first giving him her heart.

More than anything, she wanted to tell him that she *did* want to marry him. Had since he'd stolen her breath that day at Esherton Green when he'd descended from his coach, his face wreathed in smiles and the sun had glinted off his golden head. It had taken her a while to identify the unaccustomed comfortable feeling.

Maybe someday a man and woman would be permitted to marry simply because they loved each other, and the ridiculousness of class and station and birth wouldn't matter.

Those trivialities *shouldn't* have mattered.

Two souls merging—only that was essential, not the rest of the folderol.

Summoning every speck of courage she possessed, she'd determinedly shoved her heritage and reservations aside, and if Alex asked her again, she'd brave the repercussions, seize love with both hands, and say yes.

Yes, she would gladly marry him. Yes, she wanted him in the ways a woman wants a man.

Yes, she'd face the censure; take the risks loving someone beyond reason entailed. Yes, she would be his for all time.

Except he'd rushed to dismiss her, curtailing her bumbling pronouncement, almost as if he'd feared what she might say. As if he hadn't wanted to hear it.

Doubt, sinister and accusing then raised its troll-like head, and she'd feared Alex's rejection.

Uncertainty plagued her yet this morning, and she hated her misgivings.

She tongued a dab of sweet cream from the cup's rim then licked her sticky lips.

Alex's disquiet wasn't because he hadn't been as aroused as she or hadn't enjoyed their encounter. Raised around livestock, she knew what the insistent bump nudging her bum was. True, genuine concern about being discovered might have prompted him to dismiss her, but something in his demeanor, a leeriness, fairly shouted that something else had brought on his reluctance.

So now, mortified to her soles, she contemplated her next step. Staying underneath the same roof as Alex?

No, too unthinkably awkward.

She couldn't ask Heath to boot him to the pavement without raising suspicion either.

Besides, she didn't want Alex and Heath's friendship jeopardized. Nonetheless, living in the same house as Alex, was impossible. Imprudent too. God knew what mortifying thing she might do next.

Propose to him? Climb into his bed?

The latter rather appealed. Tremendously.

However, until she came of age, Heath and Brooke wouldn't hear of her assuming her own residence. But, would they permit her to winter in the country perhaps? Hadn't she been dreading that very thing mere weeks ago? What a reversal.

She snorted, startling Freddy.

He blinked sleepily before lowering his head and resuming his nap. Time to think logically and sensibly.

If she hired a companion, say someone older, respectable—mayhap a widow—might she pursue relocating to her house on Belgrave Square? Yes, a companion. The idea possessed real merit. But the woman couldn't be stuffy, pompous, or mousy.

Brette tapped her fingernails against the bone china, the soft clicking revealing her restlessness and resounding louder than it ought to have in the quiet room.

Had Mr. Shipwreck unearthed anything more about her parents? Nearly a week had passed since she'd met with him, and he might have news.

She'd send a note round and ask him straight out.

No more demurring, graciously holding her tongue,

or pretending hesitancy rather than being straightforward. From this point onward, she'd speak her mind, directly ask what she wanted to know, and worry less about offending others or what they might think.

Uncrossing and then recrossing her ankles with the other leg on top, she perused the too silent drawing room. In fact, the entire house was far too quiet to suit her.

Shortly after breaking his fast, Heath had reluctantly left Brooke to attend to urgent business. Brooke rested in her chamber, and if Alex stayed true to his word, he was yet abed sleeping off his excess drink.

Even in his cups, he'd been a dashed attractive rogue.

The servants scuttled about, whispering and tiptoeing, probably on Jenkin's orders. The poor butler had gone chalk white when Heath had carried Brooke into the manor, and as certain as Freddy was a gaseous bundle of fur, Jenkin would personally ensure Brooke's convalescence remained undisturbed. No hint of anything remotely unsettling would reach her ears.

Bored to her black-slippered toes, Brette yawned. Mayhap she should ask a footman or maid to accompany her on a brisk walk. Anything to occupy her mind and exercise always helped lessen any tension.

She sneezed then sneezed again. Blowing her nose, she eyed the crisp outdoors. A walk mightn't be the best idea after all. She suspected she'd caught a slight cold—nothing much more than a sniffly nose and few sneezes. Not wishing to expose the children, she'd sent word she wouldn't visit the foundling home until she recovered. Likely her escapade on the freezing terrace last night hadn't helped her health either.

A humorless smile tipped her mouth.

After kissing Alex, she'd probably given the illness to him too.

How could they explain that awkwardness? The only two in the household with colds?

As she swallowed the last sip of savory cocoa, she perused the lane once more. A familiar young man—one of Mr. Shipwreck's clerks? Possibly the carroty-headed chap—bundled to his red-tipped ears trotted up the front steps, his breaths forming tiny, frozen clouds before him.

A few moments later, Jenkin entered the drawing room, bearing a salver. "A note has arrived for you, Miss."

Wonderful. The messenger had been Mr. Shipwreck's clerk. Hopefully he brought the news she coveted.

"Thank you, Jenkin." She accepted the missive

before placing her empty cup on the chocolate service.

Jenkin tucked the small silver tray beneath an arm. "Shall I remove the chocolate now, Miss?"

"Yes, please." Examining the letter—indeed from the solicitor's office—she inclined her head distractedly. She cracked the seal and swiftly scanned the contents.

Too polite to ask what the missive contained, Jenkin lifted the hot chocolate tray. "Do you require anything else?"

"Yes, a carriage brought round immediately. My solicitor has asked me to visit his office at my earliest convenience." She refolded the note. "And when Brooke awakens, or if Lord Ravensdale returns, will you please tell them I've gone to Mr. Shipwreck's, but I'll return before luncheon?"

"Very good, Miss. Which maid will you take with you?"

"Flora. Tell her we're to leave in the next five minutes." Flora, a trifle slow in the attic, wasn't as essential to the running of the house as the other servants. She'd been with the Culpeppers for the past decade, and when Brooke married Heath, she'd insisted the maid join his household. Inordinately kind, Jenkin assigned Flora simple tasks that kept her busy but didn't overly challenge her.

A few minutes later, Brette hurried along the corridor. As she reached Alex's room, she slowed to a stop. Lifting her hand, she bit her lip. No. She mustn't. Unmarried women didn't knock upon unmarried gentlemen's bedchamber doors. Besides, what would she say?

I enjoyed our passionate encounter last night, and I'd like to repeat it. Now. Tonight. For the rest of my life.

She continued to her room, and after swiftly exchanging her slippers for half-boots and collecting a warm wrap, bonnet, and muff, retraced her steps.

Still no sign of Alex. He truly wasn't accustomed to strong drink.

Twenty minutes later, wearing a fur-lined midnight blue mantle over her pelisse, Brette accepted the coachman's hand as he assisted her from the coach. Frigid air smacked her in the face, and she sucked in an involuntary breath. Hounds' teeth but it was cold. She eyed the leaden November sky. Snow before afternoon or she wasn't blond. Terribly unusual for this time of year.

"Thank you, Peters."

She stuck her head into the vehicle's interior, where Flora sat bundled in several lap robes, her feet resting on a hot brick.

Flora sneezed into her handkerchief three times. A cold too?

Well, at least if Alex did become ill, no one would find it unusual now.

"Flora, why don't you stay in here? I expect I'll be done in less than thirty minutes. Peters can pick up the items I need while I'm with the solicitor, and you can assist him by remaining with the packages."

"Oh, yes, Miss. Thank you, Miss." Her face flushed and eyes watery, Flora sniffed loudly and burrowed deeper into the robe's folds. Yes, most definitely not feeling up to snuff.

Neither could Brette ask the maid to stop at the alchemist and glover when Flora already felt sickly and should seek her bed as soon as possible.

His hand resting on one of the horse's broad rump, Peters scrutinized the barren lane.

In the distance, a pair of riders clopped along as a single vehicle rattled over the cobblestones. Quiet for a weekday morning, but the bitingly frigid temperature and the promise of rare snow doubtless accounted for the lack of activity.

An indistinguishable breed of quaking ducks flew overhead, their ebony bodies' mere shadows against the pewter sky. In a typical vee formation, their wings beating frantically, they veered toward the river.

Probably wintering on the Thames. If Brette could manage the housing situation to her benefit, she'd be wintering in London too.

She eyed a smart black coach as it leisurely trundled by Heath's. She'd need a conveyance if her plans came to fruition; a phaeton or curricle would do. In a bold and daring color. Maybe the same brilliant shade of blue as her mantle. Wouldn't that be something? So regal. She'd need horseflesh, too. A matched pair—gray or white—and a mount for riding. A small, gentle mare ought to suffice.

Brette handed the driver her short list. "Here are the items I need, Peters."

"Are you certain, Miss Culpepper? His lordship won't like me leaving you." Most endearing, Peter's consternation and loyalty.

"I shall be fine. You'll be back before I'm finished or soon thereafter. The businesses I need you to frequent are a mere block or two away. Do ask the alchemist for extra elderberry and yarrow." They'd be needed if more of the household took ill with the cold. She veered Flora a glance. "And I don't want Flora to have to sit in Mr. Shipwreck's outer office. The chairs look terribly uncomfortable, and it's rather chilly."

Peters shuffled his feet and fiddled with the list, his indecision apparent.

"I'll take full responsibility, Peters." What could possibly happen? "Wait until I'm in the establishment before you leave." Surely, no one could object to her visiting her solicitor in broad daylight. She wasn't likely to have arranged a lovers' tryst in his drab office, for pity's sake.

Brette shoved her other hand into her muff. The unseasonably cold weather made her anxious for the lined gloves Peters was to pick up on her behalf. Though the muff kept her hands warm, she couldn't do anything while using it, and when she didn't, her fingers grew red from cold.

"Very well, but promise you'll stay inside until I return." He shut the coach's door. "Sometimes the traffic's difficult, and I might be a few minutes later than expected to collect you."

"I promise." Raising her muff in farewell, she hurried up the steps. Once within the brick building, she stood on her toes and peeked out the square, dusty window beside the door. Peters settled himself in the driver's seat. With a sharp whistle and a practiced snap of his whip, the team surged onward.

Best get to it. Brette didn't want him returning before she'd completed her business. Her stomach constricted as she walked the short corridor's distance. She wasn't altogether certain she wanted to know what was so urgent the solicitor couldn't tell her in the note.

After last night's disappointing incident with Alex, as well as the scare with Brooke, she didn't relish another upset. Taking a bracing breath, she forced her mouth upward and stepped into the office.

"Miss Culpepper." Mr. Loomis leaped to his feet, bumping his desk in his haste and jolting his inkwell and candle holder. The candle tipped precariously, and he grabbed the taper, steadying it. He hastily ran one hand across his wiry hair and tugged at his rumpled coat with the other.

"To what do we owe this unexpected pleasure?"

Hold this truth close to your heart and remember its perils: We leniently judge ourselves by our intentions, while harshly judging others by their behaviors.
~*Appearances and Attitude—The Genteel Lady's Guide to Practical Living*

13

A lex flipped his pocket watch open and grinned. Not even half past seven. Excellent.

He'd enjoyed the invigorating walk here, despite the brisk cold, his lack of sleep, and a head which felt swollen twice its normal size. He'd made excellent time too. Never mind he could scarcely feel his fingers and toes.

Sliding his timepiece into his pocket, he chuckled.

Grandmama didn't rise before ten. The old bird would have a conniption fit upon hearing he'd called this early. And the fuss she'd kick up when she learned why he'd put in an early appearance—

He grinned in anticipation.

'Twould serve his meddlesome grandmother right. Hopefully, the early hour would have her a mite more compliant and her tongue less caustic. He rapped the door knocker three times then, for good measure, banged it twice more, wincing as an answering peal jolted within his skull.

Served *him* right for over-indulging last night.

Last night. Brette. His beautiful, desirable Brette.

His behavior had confused her, but he'd set everything aright today.

Determination to put his grandmother straight had him dressed and shaved by six. He intended to inform her in no uncertain terms precisely what unpleasantness she could expect if she defied him or spread any more slanderous rumors regarding Brette.

After last night, nothing could persuade him his sweet Brette didn't share his feelings. He must somehow convince her to admit it, and to realize that neither of them would ever be happy without the other.

Nothing and no one else mattered.

He pounded the entry with his fist then clapped the knocker several more times. *Answer the door!* His head threatened to burst, and his hollow stomach objected by turning flips. He swallowed. Mayhap he should have delayed long enough to drink a cup—or pot—of coffee and eaten a small repast.

Norris, Grandmama's butler, still shoving an arm in his cutaway, opened the door. A whole two inches.

From his elevated bushy eyebrows to his mouth cinched tighter than purse strings, he radiated displeasure. "My lord," he droned, annoyance accenting each word, "the dowager countess is yet abed. Please return at a more civilized hour."

Norris made to shut the door, but Alex wasn't having it. He shoved his boot into the crack, grimacing as his toes suffered a nasty pinch.

Norris's incredulous eyebrows scampered higher on his forehead.

"*Tsk*, is that any way to welcome a guest?" Smiling reproachfully, Alex shouldered his way inside. "You do know, don't you, Norris, who now pays your wages?"

Didn't hurt to remind the sour-faced servant that Alex expected civility. Particularly to the chap Norris owed his position to.

"Indeed, sir," Norris replied, stiffer than the flooring they stood upon and about as amiable as an angry scorpion. His head barely reached Alex's shoulder yet Norris managed to look down his nose disdainfully while extending his hand.

"I thought so." Alex passed the butler his hat, cane, and gloves before removing his greatcoat and scarf and handing them over. "Good man."

Not wishing to give Grandmama anything else to quibble about, he'd donned mourning togs for his visit.

Straightening his coat's rumpled cuff, Alex perused the entry. Each stick of furniture, the paintings, the decorations—everything right down to the crocheted and tatted doilies—were in precisely the same location they had been for at least two decades.

If nothing else, Grandmama remained consistent and predictable. Rigidly immovable in attitudes and habits too. She probably still slept with those damnable cats. Temperamental, pampered beasts.

The last time he'd called, Ambrosia had jumped onto his shoulder and tried to steal his biscuit, right from his mouth. The determined, portly feline had batted his face, her claws extended, when he'd not shared a nibble. The other, younger one, Emerald—named for her eye color—had hissed and given him an open-mouthed sneer each time he moved.

He much preferred dogs. They knew who their master was.

After hanging up Alex's coat, Norris, his posture taut with indignation, preceded him up the stairs. "If you will please make yourself comfortable in the parlor, my lord, I shall inform Madame you are here."

He said it with as much enthusiasm as at the prospect of waking an ill-tempered dragon. Not too far off, by God.

Alex didn't miss the butler failing to offer him

refreshments. Or, perhaps, fretting about Grandmama's reaction to an early morning caller, the courtesy had slipped his mind.

"That's all right. I'll surprise her." Too much to hope Norris might have a battle shield tucked away somewhere. A sword and helmet? Perchance a garlic clove?

No, no, that deters vampires. Not crotchety, intrusive grandmothers.

Slack-jawed and gaping, Norris spread his arms wide and flapped them in an attempt to block the corridor.

Giant, agitated penguin.

God help me keep a straight face. Please.

Alex sidestepped the flummoxed butler.

"But, sir, you mustn't. Her ladyship—"

"First door on the right, isn't it?" Alex patted Norris's extended arm as he passed. Norris scampered to catch up. "Yes, but, you cannot simply—"

"I thought so." Alex lengthened his stride.

"M'lord. I must insist. She's nae at her best first thin'." In his desperation, Norris had forgotten his polished speech and reverted to Scots.

Truly overwrought, poor chap. He'd shrink in mortification should he become aware of the slip. Was Grandmama so formidable her staff lived in dread of displeasing her?

Yes.

Alex cast the butler a compassionate glance, but didn't slow his pace. "Break your fast, Norris. I'd hate to think you went hungry on my account. And trust me, you would rather be elsewhere when my grandmother hears what I have to say."

The faithful servant paused.

He wavered, one troubled eye on the closed door, behind which the distinct echo of Grandmama's snoring resounded. Or else a cantankerous walrus with a vigorous head cold resided in her bedchamber. With a regal tilt of his head, Norris consented. "Very good, my lord. Please ring should you or her ladyship need anything."

Wise chap. Undoubtedly far wiser than Alex. "Norris?"

Several feet along the passage already, as if terrified of Grandmama waking and finding him outside her chamber, he swung to face Alex. "Yes, sir?"

"I commend you for your diligence and loyalty." Alex grasped the door handle. With a slight dip of his head, Norris accepted the compliment then made his escape.

Alex waited until the butler descended the stairs before knocking loudly as he threw open the door.

"Happy morning to you, Grandmama!"

Whistling a cheerful, uncouth sailor's tune, certain to peeve her, he yanked the thick curtains wide, revealing the rotund tabbies sleeping on either side of her legs. Frost covered the window panes, but no coal burned in her hearth.

Positively freezing in here.

"Alexander?" she mumbled sleepily, her mountain of bedcovers rustling as she sat up, her lacy night cap askew.

He'd truly surprised her if she'd slipped and called him by his given name.

She blinked drowsily while covering a less than delicate yawn. "Whatever are you doing here?" Alarm flitted across her aged face, and she pressed her hands to her lavender, ruffle-clad chest. "Has something happened? It has. I can see it in your eyes. Don't spare me, Wycombe. Tell me all."

Much too early for such theatrics.

"No, Grandmama, nothing has happened except I learned last evening that you're propagating rumors that Miss Culpepper's mother was a whore." Alex bent and attended to the grate. Couldn't have her taking a chill.

Instantly defensive, his grandmother *harrumphed* and relaxed against her buttercup-yellow silk pillows. "*I* didn't start the rumors, my boy."

"Perhaps, but you will cease spreading them and encourage others to do so as well." Once he'd started the fire, he straightened and replaced the poker. He brushed his hands together, but traces of coal dust remained on his fingertips.

"Did Norris let you in? I'll sack him today, the wretch." One gnarled, blue-veined hand petting Ambrosia, Grandmama glared at Alex.

He'd inherited her vivid green eyes, but now looking into the squinted and hostile gaze, he didn't much treasure the gift. His patience near at an end, Alex shook his head, warning her with his gaze. "No, you won't. I but reminded him who pays his wages."

"How utterly common and vulgar."

Yes, better to pretend the staff's wages magically appear from another realm, delivered by a Scottish faerie each month.

She sniffed and curled her lip. "As is calling at this ungodly hour and barging into my private chamber."

"Prepare yourself for even worse crassness. Shall I get your salts in case you faint?" He made a pretense of searching her dressing table for the vial.

"*Pshaw*. Don't be ridiculous. I do not swoon, and I doubt what you say will shock me overly much." Her bravado didn't reach her eyes. Wariness tinged the wrinkled edges. "Out with it."

Arms folded, he relaxed against a gold and purple satin-festooned bedpost. "If you don't cease persecuting Miss Culpepper, I shall cut off your funds and refuse to pay your bills henceforth."

Her jaw sagged for an instant, but she recovered almost as quickly. "You—"

He sharply raised his palm, halting her protest. "Don't say something you'll regret later, Grandmama, for I do not threaten idly."

Hurling him a mutinous glower, she snapped her mouth shut, her teeth clacking with her ire.

She folded her arms, peevishly tapping one arm with her bony fingers.

She's fairly frothing to lay into me.

"I'm sure in recent weeks you've considered your situation. Once I marry, the countess is entitled to the dowager house, and I doubt, given the enmity between you, she'll invite you to remain." He fingered the bed curtain's gold tassel, letting the truth of his words sink in.

She made a rough noise in the back of her throat, but kept her lips firmly pinched together. "Without funds, you'll be reduced to living with one of my sisters." Resolute, Alex didn't spare her. "Most likely rotated between their three households since you make yourself so disagreeable to everyone. I'd much rather you continued in comfort, able to travel and visit as you are inclined to, instead of living at the mercy of others' generosity and whims."

Grandmama averted her gaze, the first traces of vulnerability he'd observed softening her wrinkled face. Dropping her focus to the bedsheet, she plucked at the frayed lace edge. "You've mulled this through, I see."

He sank onto the bed and clasped her cool hand. "I don't want to do this to you, Grandmama. Though you can be difficult and petty, and you seldom have a kind thing to say, I do love you."

Her wide green eyes sought his, and a trace of warmth glimmered in their depths. "You do?"

The two shaky words held such disbelief and hope, his heart softened. "I do. You're the matriarch of our family, and I think if you'd put aside your prickly exterior, you'd find my sisters want to love you too." He kissed her knobby knuckles.

She blinked back tears, and her voice cracked. "I'd ... like that. I've been lonely."

"I know you have, and I want to remedy that. But I adore Brette. I shall do everything I can to win her heart. She's beautiful, kind, and intelligent, and she has the most delightful laugh." *And a delectable bottom and bosoms.* "Her background and pedigree don't matter an iota to me, and I'd much prefer your blessing than a rift between us. However, the choice is yours, Grandmama. I'll not be dissuaded."

Grandmama's lower lip trembled, and she withdrew her hand to collect a handkerchief from her nightstand. A frail, uncertain old woman had replaced the grand, imposing dame. She dabbed the corners of her eyes.

"I understand." She gave him a wobbly half-smile. "A lifetime of habits is difficult to break, and I may need a little time to adjust, but I intend to try. Truly. You will have to bear with me. Please."

"That's all I ask." Emerald crawled onto his lap, and Alex eyed her warily. He held his breath lest she remember her dislike of him. Instead of arching her spine and hissing, she closed her eyes and started purring.

"I think she likes you." Grandmama gave him a tremulous smile, though moisture still glinted in her eyes.

"She detested me the last time I was here. Wanted to use me as a human claw-sharpener." He arched a brow and whispered, "I'm entirely too terrified to move."

"Emerald's accepted you now. You needn't fear.'" She exhaled loudly as she wiped her nose. "Wycombe, how goes the investigation into the fire? Unbearably tragic, and someone dares hint you might have been responsible? Reprehensible."

Back to Wycombe, are we?

"Heard about that, did you?" Alex ran a hand along the cat's spine.

Grandmama's lips turned up the merest bit, her familiar confidence once more in place.

"I have my sources. Actually, Wilma Wobsley mentioned it at supper last evening whilst we dined at Lady Honeycutt's. You think *I'm* difficult. At times, Martha Honeycutt makes Satan look like an inexperienced schoolboy. And Mrs. Wobsley is incapable of keeping the smallest, most trivial of secrets. A woman with a looser tongue or less common sense doesn't exist."

"Perhaps you ought to consider new friends? We are known by the company we keep, aren't we?" He braved scratching Emerald's shoulders, relaxing when she made no attempt to impale his fingers with her teeth or claws.

"Yes, after last evening, I'm of the same mind." She placed her damp handkerchief on the nightstand and prompted, "The fire?"

"Fret not. I have an irrefutable alibi, and I've hired runners to look into the matter for me. In fact, The Bow Street Agency is my next stop this morning. They've already uncovered my accuser. As I suspected, a disgruntled relative. A third cousin who thought nothing of falsely blaming me so he could inherit." Alex scratched behind the cat's ears, and her rumblings grew louder. "Also, a footman's gone missing, and I think that's cause for suspicion."

"Let me guess which ratty cousin. Maximillian?" she suggested, her tone dryer than charred parchment. "Envious churl. Always has been. That's one thing I always appreciated about you. You were never jealous of Arthur."

"True. I didn't envy him at all. I don't think he was altogether happy."

The fire's heat slowly spread, easing the worst of the room's nippiness. His grandmother shouldn't be sleeping in this cold environment. On his way out, he'd speak to Norris and increase the household budget to accommodate more fuel.

Come to think of it, perhaps what Alex had assumed was her preference for sameness wasn't brought about by inflexibility or habit, but rather financial necessity.

He examined her chamber with a more critical regard.

Though her room was tidy and elegantly decorated, the furnishing—everything, truth to tell—was far past its prime. Even her night cap and gown showed signs of wear. Precisely how much had Wycombe allotted her monthly?

Had Alex misjudged her circumstances?

He hadn't yet examined High Wycombe's books. Hertford, his new steward, had found the estate records a confounded muddle. Best contact him and at the very least determine Grandmama's current allowance.

"Alexander?" Her unease tangible, she brushed a silvery lock off her pale forehead. "Yes?"

She hesitated, as if torn.

He patted her hand. "You can tell me. It can't be as bad as all that."

Grandmama scooted back, dragging Ambrosia onto her lap. "I heard something else last night I think you ought to know, though I'm not sure what you can do about it."

Progress already. An hour ago, she'd not have taken him into her confidence.

Setting the cat aside, he stood. He must run multiple errands before returning to Highfield and seeking Brette. He brushed cat hair from his trousers and coat. Times like this, he wished a valet awaited him to attend to the task later. Perhaps after he settled the estate's finances.

Looks like I rolled in the stuff.

He continued to pick long, gray cat hairs from his person. "It concerns your Miss Culpepper."

"How so?" His unease spiraled upward, and he left off ridding his garments of feline fur. Emerald rolled onto her back, presenting her plump belly for petting. Grandmama obliged, scraping her fingers across the cat's round tummy. "I don't know if you are aware, but Wilma Wobsley is the newest Duchess of Bellinghamshire's mother. She claims Bellinghamshire petitioned for Miss Culpepper's guardianship."

Alex froze. "Pardon?"

Conniving blackguard. This changes everything.

"According to Wilma, the Bellinghamshires are desperate for the funds they presumed their Genevia would inherit, and have borrowed heavily against her inheritance. The duke plans on marrying Miss Culpepper off immediately upon being granted the guardianship. There's something about an agreement with her intended allowing them to keep half her inheritance. I'm not positive the arrangement's even legal."

Hounds' teeth!

The prospect hadn't occurred to him. Or Raven, he'd wager. And it surely wouldn't have to Brette. "Her inheritance can't be substantial enough that they'd stoop to those means. Didn't the duke inherit the bulk when he came into the title?"

"I'm not altogether sure. I seem to recall the eldest son had a falling out with Fusty Boots. In any event, his grace has already arranged a match with—" Grandmama shuddered delicately. "God help me, I can hardly bear to say it."

Blood boiling, Alex gritted his teeth. How dare the Bellinghamshires treat Brette like an expendable pawn to gain her piddly inheritance? Undulating waves of unaccustomed rage knotted his gut and thrummed through him. "Who's she promised to?"

Grandmama wrinkled her nose and puckered her lips as if forced to eat wriggling maggots. "The Marquis Duplesse."

No!

"That sod? He's ailing too, isn't he? He's also an unconscionable reprobate, and he's ancient. Seventy, if he's a day." Too much drink and whoring. He'd gone through three wives already. By God, the blackguard would likely infect Brette with the clap or worse.

Grandmama arched him a starchy glance. "I beg your pardon?"

"Don't get your feathers ruffled, Grandmama. You remain inarguably exquisite, but he's a debauched blackguard, fifty years Brette's senior." Alex yanked the bell. He needed to be away, and he wanted a word with

Norris first.

"He's nearer eighty, and I think the Bellinghamshires hope he'll die soon, so they can barter your Miss Culpepper again." She shook her head, and her cap slipped lower onto her forehead. "I wouldn't wish that fate on the girl, no matter her background." She shot him a repentant glance. "I didn't mean to sound judgmental."

Alex managed a distracted half-smile.

Musings banged louder than a tinker's wagon in his already sensitive skull. He wasn't ever downing more than a finger's worth of spirits again.

He raked a hand through his hair. What to do first?

Speak to Raven? Acquire a special license? Meet with the Bow Street investigators? Inquire if Brette's solicitor would speak with him? Trot by the Chancery Court and poke around to determine how far the guardianship request had progressed? Hightail it to Highfield Place House and propose?

Again?

He'd have to borrow Grandmama's coach. Besides the sullen weather discouraging further foot travel, he had no time to spare. On second thought, he'd better collect a special license first. He wouldn't put anything past Bellinghamshire, and Alex wasn't chancing Brette falling into the duke's clutches.

"Alexander. I think I understand how much you care for the girl, but the matter's out of your hands." True remorse made her voice husky. Or his grandmother was an accomplished actress.

No, her concern rang sincere. She hadn't had to share this news with him and in doing so, she'd revealed a change of heart.

"There's no help for it. I'll have to wed Brette by special license as soon as possible." He bent and kissed her cheek. "I would be honored if you'd attend."

"But ... but you're in mourning," she stammered, sitting up and setting the cat aside in her astonishment. "You cannot marry right now. Proprieties must be observed, Wycombe. What will people say?"

Ah, a tinge of censure there.

"If I wait, Brette may be forced to marry Dupresse, and that's far worse than temporarily miffing the *ton* sensibilities. I'm an earl. They'll forgive me. Marrying during a mourning period is neither illegal nor immoral, merely frowned upon."

"You've been spared the *haut ton*'s censure. I assure you, it's most unpleasant." Issuing a resigned sigh, she sagged into her pillows once more. "But, I shall support you. I think Miss Culpepper is a charming girl, and I hope she'll forgive me for my earlier churlishness. Nonetheless, you ought to warn her that at times I can be a trifle obstinate and opinionated."

At times?

"I'm sure you will get on famously. At least I hope so, for I would love for you to live with us, if you are inclined to." Though Grandmama had sworn she'd try, he didn't expect an overnight transformation. Luckily, Brette possessed a forgiving nature.

Tears seeped from his Grandmother's eyes, trailing onto her crepey cheeks. "Truly, Alexander? After I've been so difficult?"

"Truly. But you will be kind to Brette. Promise me."

"I shall, dear, I promise."

A soft rap echoed at the door.

"Come." Grandmama looked expectantly at the entrance.

Her abigail, wearing a severe brown gown and bearing a tray, scooted into the bedchamber. "I took the liberty of bringing your breakfast early, my lady." She sent Alex a nervous, sideways glance. "Since someone rang the bell."

"Very well done of you, Kingstone." Grandmama shoved another pillow behind her back. "I am anticipating my tea this morning. Rising early does invigorate one's appetite." She eagerly lifted the silver dome. "Kippers and ham. Splendid."

"I'll be on my way." Alex strode to the door, determined to apprise Brette of the situation first and worry about the rest of his pressing concerns once she'd agreed to marry him. "Would you mind terribly if I borrowed your coach. I walked here."

Grandmama fluttered her fingers at him. "Indeed. Just inform Norris. I haven't anywhere to go before two o'clock today. Oh, I nearly forgot, dear boy."

Dear boy, am I now? Such miraculous progress already.

Teacup poised at her mouth, she paused. "Bellinghamshire has a man watching the young lady. Following her. Wilma was particularly giddy about the fact. He means to..." She cast a practiced eye at her rapt abigail, who promptly applied herself to selecting Grandmama's clothing for the day. "...remove her from her family's care. Says he has the legal right."

Noble intentions alone are not enough:
Commitment, sacrifice, and even the smallest
of actions are more powerful and longer lasting.
~Appearances and Attitude—The Genteel Lady's
Guide to Practical Living

14

*U*nexpected?

The coppery-haired clerk gave Brette a shy smile, and, tucking her fur muff beneath one arm, she answered with a friendly smile.

"I received a note from Mr. Shipwreck asking me to attend him at my earliest convenience."

In the corner, a smallish, pot-bellied stove beckoned, and she crossed the floor's worn planks to warm her hands. She might have saved the effort. The pathetic amount of heat radiating from the under-stoked iron wouldn't have cooked an egg much less boil the water in the dented kettle sitting on a side table with the makings for tea.

Mr. Shipwreck didn't seem miserly, but his help suffered from the cold. Wise leaving Flora in the carriage. She'd have been miserable.

"A note? From this office?" Completely baffled, hands on his hips, the secretary cocked his head before pointing an accusatory stare at each clerk in turn.

Angling her shoulders to the humble stove, Brette dipped her head, indicating the redheaded chap. "Yes. I believe your young man there delivered it."

"I did, along with the other correspondences, as Pauly and I do each morning." A troubled frown crinkled the youth's forehead.

Which of the other clerks was Pauly?

Ah, the expressionless fellow. He slowly blinked at her before applying his quill to whatever he'd diligently been working on before she interrupted.

"And a letter for Miss Culpepper was included in the missives?" Mr. Loomis demanded, peevishly sucking in his cheeks,

The redhead dared a reluctant nod.

"Well, obviously, or I wouldn't be here." Brette conjured her most reassuring smile and attempted levity.

Her efforts fell flat.

Throwing his hands up, the secretary made no effort to conceal his flustered state. "Goodness me. How am I to properly perform my duties if I'm not apprised of the goings-on in this office? Notes being delivered hither and yon, and not as much as a by your leave to me. Unacceptable, I tell you."

"If it's an inconvenient time, I can return later—" Which meant she'd have to wait longer to learn what Mr. Shipwreck had discovered. Drat it all. Besides, no coach waited outside, and she'd have to sit here until it returned.

The inner door swung open, and Mr. Shipwreck, papers in hand and spectacles barely clinging to the end of his nose, poked his head out. "Loomis, I shall need—"

He caught sight of Brette beside the stove, appearing only slightly less astonished than Mr. Loomis at her seeing her in his office. He, however, recovered much more adroitly.

This is very peculiar.

"Ah, Miss Culpepper. I'm glad you've stopped in."

You sent for me.

"I have important news for you."

Hence your summons.

Shoving his eyeglasses up his nose, he perused the room, his bafflement almost comedic. "You're alone?"

"My maid remained in the coach. She's not feeling well." No need to tell him the conveyance wasn't parked before his establishment.

"Come in, please." He stepped aside and indicated

she should enter his office. "Loomis, I'll need Miss Culpepper's file, and for heaven's sake, add coal to the stove. How can the staff possibly work if they're half frozen? Prepare the chaps a spot of tea too. Their cheeks and noses are almost as red as Mr. Jacobson's hair."

An exaggeration there. The chamber wasn't *that* cold.

"Yes, sir. Right away, sir. I saw the file this morning. It's here somewhere." Mr. Loomis immediately started riffling through the folders neatly stacked atop his desk, muttering the whole while. "Might've informed me. Can't expect me to read minds. How's a body to perform their job? Perfectly warm enough for me. Can't be pampering the help."

As Brette entered the cozier room, she pressed her lips together to check her smile.

Mr. Shipwreck rolled his eyes ceilingward as he shut the door behind them. "He's as fussy as an old tabby, but meticulously organized, if a mite miserly. And frankly, I couldn't function without him."

After seeing her to a chair, he settled himself behind his desk, folded his hands, and gave her a rather jovial smile. Ink stained the fingertips of his right hand, and his coat appeared as if he'd slept in it. "I finished my notes on your situation last night and intended to send a letter 'round to Lord Ravensdale this morning asking him to bring you by. You saved me the trouble."

"But, Mr. Shipwreck, I received a missive from you this morning." She rummaged in her reticule and, after finding the crisply folded square, passed it to him.

His eyebrows jumped to his receding hairline and hung there suspended as he unfolded the letter. Shaking his head, he thrust the foolscap her way. "I assure you, I didn't write this."

Unease, like a cold, clammy snake, slithered down the length of Brette's spine. The obvious question, *"Who had then?"* pealed loudly in her head.

A sharp rap preceded Mr. Loomis's entrance. He bore the file, holding it reverently as if he carried the crown jewels. "Would you care for a cup of tea, Miss Culpepper? The kettle's already on. I concede, it's a brisk one outside today. Think it will snow? I don't ever recall snow in November before."

Though rattled by Mr. Shipwreck's disclosure, Brette managed to muster a smile for the eager-to-please man. "That's kind of you, but no tea for me, thank you. And, yes, I do believe we should prepare for at least a smattering of snow."

As soon as Mr. Loomis exited, she bent across the desk and collected the letter. "This was delivered by your clerk. The red-haired fellow—"

"Elias Jacobson," the solicitor offered, his

countenance as baffled as hers must've been. "He's a trustworthy chap, too." He rubbed his jaw, eyes partially closed in contemplation. "I cannot imagine where it came from. Most disturbing, and I assure you, I shall have an answer from my staff. Entirely unacceptable—slipping correspondences into my posts." He pointed to the letter. "It's going to cost someone their position, I can tell you."

Had Alex's grandmother bribed a clerk to lure Brette from the house? The dowager countess didn't know Heath wouldn't accompany her. Unless his urgent summons this morning had been part of the ploy too. To make sure he wasn't at home when Brette received the writ.

Bother and rot.

Either Brette's imagination was running amok, or she'd played right into the manipulating woman's hands. What could the old crow hope to accomplish? Blessedly dedicated, Peters couldn't be bribed. There'd be no forgetting to collect her or delivering her to the wrong address. Nevertheless, prudence demanded she send a note to Highfield and inquire if Raven or Alex, or even a footman or two, could convey her home. No sense taking undue chances.

If the dowager was responsible, she had some nerve, and Brette fully intended to inform Alex. Surely, she'd listen to her grandson. As the earl, he headed the family now.

Do you remember her behavior the other day? Does she seem like a dutiful woman?

Pasting a deliberately cheery smile on her face, Brette placed her beaded reticule beside her ermine muff on Mr. Shipwreck's desk. "I'd like to send a note to Highfield, requesting an escort home. Could I trouble you for a piece of foolscap and a quill? While I wait, we can discuss whatever news you have for me."

"I'm in agreement. I think an escort is wise." He pushed an inkwell and quill across the once shiny desktop.

"My driver is running errands for me, otherwise I'd have him deliver the request." In short order, Brette wrote the note and Mr. Shipwreck entrusted it to Mr. Loomis for delivery. "Please deliver this straightaway, and await a response."

"Very good, miss." In a rush, the secretary bustled from the office, and in his haste, overlooked closing the door snugly behind him. "Pauly, quickly man," Mr. Loomis ordered, his reedy voice carrying into the inner office. "This letter needs delivering to Highfield Place House promptly. You're to wait for a response. No dawdling to and from, either, if you value your position. You've pages of documents to copy today."

"Yes, Mr. Loomis." A stool scraped across the floor, followed a few moments later by a door thudding closed.

"Now, then." The solicitor opened her file, his businesslike demeanor in place once more. "I think you'll be well-pleased at what we've managed to uncover on your behalf."

Brette's stomach tumbled giddily. "Please tell me my parents were married after all." Why did it matter so much?

"Indeed." He raised an affirmative brow and smiled broadly.

"And the ceremony was witnessed by several associates of theirs as well as a visiting cleric." He perused the papers. "A Vicar Wonderly, who's a bishop in Lincoln now."

Brette wanted to jump up, shout her joy, and dance around the room. Instead, she settled for happily wiggling her toes in her boots. "So there can be no doubt of my legitimacy?"

"None, whatsoever."

She sank back into the chair and released an extended breath. Apparently, her father hadn't been a complete rapscallion after all. "I shan't pretend I'm not delighted. It does rather wear on one to think— None of that matters now, does it?"

"No indeed. But there's more, my dear Miss Culpepper." His chestnut eyes fairly twinkled with his secret. "I suspected it might be the case, but naturally, I performed due diligence first. I needed to be certain before I approached you. It's most startling, really, but I think you will be pleased."

"Mr. Shipwreck, I cannot imagine what has you so ... exuberant." Brette laughed. "I'm sure it cannot be more staggering than discovering I'm legitimate."

"Indulge me while I refresh your memory of certain relevant facts. I want to make sure you fully appreciate your position." As he spoke, he poked through the folder, withdrawing documents every now and again.

Brette angled her head. "Yes, of course. Please go on."

"Your grandfather was the Duke of Bellinghamshire."

Old Fusty Boots.

"And your father was his second son. His grace quarreled with his eldest son, the heir, and they never reconciled. Being a spiteful codger, the old duke bequeathed his unentailed worldly possessions to the—and I quote here..." He scrutinized the parchment before him. "'...eldest

legitimate, living offspring produced from the loins of my younger sons.'" He glanced up, his mien almost smug. "There are only two surviving grandchildren, Miss Culpepper. You and one other, *younger,* granddaughter."

Heart and stomach floundering clumsily somewhere in the vicinity of her shaky knees, Brette straightened until she perched on the chair's edge.

Good Lord. He doesn't mean...?

Mr. Shipwreck beamed, his smile stretching to his ears, and his eyes crumpling like folded crepes. "You, my dear, are a very, *very* wealthy heiress with properties on three continents, a copper mine, two ships, a silk warehouse— The list goes on at length. Your grandfather might have been miserly, but he possessed a tremendous business sense. Unusual for a peer, truth to tell. Most abhor ties to commerce."

"I..." She shook her head in dazed disbelief. Had he truly declared Brette her grandfather's heir? "I honestly don't know what to say."

So many options had become possible in the blink of an eye. Including marrying Alex. Nothing could be grander.

Half an hour ago, a lowly by-blow, and now an heiress. And not any heiress, but the recognized granddaughter of the Duke of Bellinghamshire.

Her nose tickled, and she sneezed twice. "Excuse me."

"Bless you," Mr. Shipwreck said, his face still wreathed in smiles.

Fishing her hankie from her reticule, she pressed the square to her nostrils and considered her options. Perchance the house in Belgrave Square could be turned into a school. She must inspect the place. And if not, she had funds to purchase an adequate facility. "So what happens now? How do we proceed?"

"There's the uncomfortable business of informing your uncle, the current duke, that the funds and properties held in trust for his seven-year-old daughter, Genevia, are no longer hers." Mr. Shipwreck rubbed his chin. "I can't think he'll take the news well."

"Most unfair, I think." Brette fingered her reticule's strap. Another conundrum brought about by the circumstances of birth. "Couldn't I set aside a trust for her?"

Brette wasn't about to refuse this most welcome and altogether unexpected gift, but denying her cousin a portion seemed beyond selfish.

"That's generous of you, and you are free to do whatever you wish with your monies. I can draft the documents necessary." He paused, giving her a chagrined smile. "If you trust me to do so. Ravensdale, as your guardian, will have to approve, naturally."

Mr. Shipwreck had gone far and beyond to help her

determine her heritage. Unconscionable to sack him now. "Of course I trust you, and I hope you'll agree to help me determine a fair settlement for Genevia too. I don't think Heath will have an issue with me bestowing funds on the girl. She's an innocent in this."

Genevia shouldn't be penalized for being born after Brette.

"I'm afraid Bellinghamshire, the younger, is nearly as crusty a curmudgeon as his father, though without the common sense of a parsnip. The vegetable would probably do a better job of managing Bellinghamshire's monies, truth be told." Mr. Shipwreck grew more solemn, tense even, as he gave his earlobe another tug. "And you should know, he's aware of your existence. Has been for weeks now, apparently. His man of business has been snooping around, asking questions, poking his nose into your affairs."

"Should I be concerned?" For an odd reason, the cocky rider passing the house this morning came to mind. Where, exactly, had she seen the blasted horse before?

Mr. Shipwreck regarded the cracked door and scrunched his forehead. "Let me close the door before we continue."

What would Alex say when he learned of the turnabout in her station? His grandmother?

Brette didn't require or seek the dowager's approval, but now the dame had no grounds for her objections. A wicked smile threatened in anticipation of seeing the Gambwells' reactions when they learned of her good fortune. However, Brette mustn't gloat or be vindictive.

Well, a jot of reveling might be permitted where those tabbies were concerned.

After returning to his seat, Mr. Shipwreck sank heavily onto his chair. "I think caution is sensible, and I wish to speak to Ravensdale on the matter. That's why I'd hoped he'd come with you today."

"Well, perhaps he'll be the one to escort me home, and you'll have the opportunity."

"I do hope that's the case," Mr. Shipwreck murmured while thumbing through more papers in her file. "I don't recall your birthdate, Miss Culpepper. How old are you?"

Sleet lashed the window behind him, a periodic fluffy snowflake in the winter mix.

Treacherous for traffic if ice carpeted the roads. Peters might be delayed, and so might whoever took on the task of ushering her home.

"I'm twenty." And old enough to know her own mind. A notion struck, astonishing and exhilarating, and her breath hitched. She'd inherited enough to open a women's college, and offer her patronage to Alex's ragged school.

Not surprising that she still wanted to help him. Would he view her differently because her lineage had become acceptable? Difficult to say. When Society had deemed her unsuitable, Alex had still wanted to marry her, or at least he'd said he did.

Now—

Good heavens.

She might be sought after by the very elitists who'd given her the cut.

Position and wealth, once again, prevailed over decency and character. Too bad for them.

Her loyalty lay with those kind-hearted enough to include her when her heritage had been doubtful.

"And when will you be one-and-twenty?"

He certainly seemed determined on that account, didn't he? Suddenly alert, she cocked her head. "In July. The seventeenth."

He huffed out a breath, drumming his fingers atop the papers. "I'd hoped it might be sooner."

"Why? What difference does it make when I come of age?"

The room had become uncomfortably warm, and she feared she perspired in a most unladylike fashion. What had Mr. Loomis done? Dumped an entire bucket of coal into the stove? She rose to make her way to a tall window, hoping it might be slighter cooler there.

One hand on the sill, she leaned over and peered outside.

No sign of Peters yet or anyone else to accompany her home either. White already dusted the trees, buildings, and sidewalks. Given the unexpected snowfall, they'd better arrive soon, or the trip home might prove adventuresome.

She sucked in a raggedy breath, an unpleasant jolt to her middle making her stomach go wobbly. An unmarked black coach stood parked beneath a tree on the opposite side of the street—the same one from earlier?—and the horseman she'd seen riding past the house this morning spoke to its occupant.

So did the clerk Mr. Loomis had just sent to Highfield House Place.

Pauly paused, pointing at the brick building housing Mr. Shipwreck's offices, before nodding and accepting a fist-sized bag from someone inside the coach. He promptly tucked it within his coat, and with a guilty look around, ducked his head and strode away.

The weasel.

The horseman remounted, and touching his hat, also left, his horse's hooves kicking up miniature snow mounds. *This is where I've seen him before.* Right here or near Mr. Shipwreck's office almost every time she and Heath paid a visit.

Even squinting, Brette couldn't identify the coach's occupant, but she'd wager her new fortune the dowager reigned within. Pounding her cane and issuing starchy orders, glaring the whole while.

Could she see Brette?

A shadow fell across the coach's window, and her nape hair stood on end. She quickly moved away from the opening, unease tapping a rapid tempo along her spine.

So, the note delivered this morning had probably been bait to lure her here.

Brette wasn't a fribbling fool. She'd not as much as poke her nose outside this building without Heath or Alex by her side. Preferably both. Except, they didn't know she needed an escort, and due to the blackguard clerk's duplicity, they wouldn't soon either.

But Jenkin knew where she'd gone, and when Peters returned, she could send him to the house to get help. No need to work herself into a dither.

"Mr. Shipwreck?"

He peered at her above the top of his eyeglasses.

She swept her hand in the window's general direction. "Your clerk, Pauly, just accepted what I assume was a bribe from someone in a coach across the street. I'm convinced my missive will not be delivered."

Mr. Shipwreck made a disgusted noise in his throat and threw down the papers he'd been reading. Earnestness replaced his former joviality. "I shall return you home safely myself, and I think we now know who planted the false letter to you, don't we?"

She retraced her steps, inexplicably chilled. Anxiety did that to a person. "I suspect there's something you're not telling me."

"Ah... Well..." The most flustered she'd seen him, he huffed out a lengthy breath and rubbed his nose. "You might as well know, Miss Culpepper. You will soon enough, in any event."

For pity's sake. Now what?

"Bellinghamshire's man of business stopped in the day before yesterday and informed me that, over a month ago, the duke petitioned for your guardianship. As your nearest living blood relation, not to mention a ranking duke, he's likely to have the request granted."

15

Unable to sit, agitation making her edgy, Brette paced in Mr. Shipwreck's office.

Careful to stay away from the window, she folded her arms and tucked her chin to her chest. She'd removed her outer wrap, and accepted a cup of tea from a most repentant and remorseful Mr. Loomis. When Mr. Shipwreck told him of Pauly's treachery, the secretary had become so distraught, she'd feared him on the brink of an apoplexy.

Mr. Loomis had promptly sent Jacobson out the rear entry, a letter secreted in his pocket, and a coal bucket in his hand. No matter that the coal bin practically overflowed. Mr. Shipwreck had provided Jacobson with funds to hire a hack a block or two away. No one should have to walk to Highfield in this miserable weather.

She puffed out her cheeks and turned to march in the other direction. What a deuced bumblebroth. Just informed she was an heiress, and mere moments later, learning her greedy uncle intended to rip her from her family.

Venturing near the window, she peeked outside. Snow steadily sifted from the sky now.

"The carriage remains there." Probably not the dowager herself, but a hireling. "And mine hasn't returned yet. I cannot imagine what the delay is, unless Peters is having difficulty negotiating the roads because of the snow."

"I'm prepared to leave with you as soon as he arrives." Mr. Shipwreck set his quill aside. "Unless we have word from Highfield before then."

"There's absolutely no way to prevent Bellinghamshire from this quest?" Brette returned to the chair she'd thrown her mantle over.

Mr. Shipwreck slumped into his chair and removed his spectacles. He rummaged in his coat pocket, and after withdrawing a handkerchief, set about polishing the glass.

"As to that, Miss Culpepper, I've been thinking, and I believe there are a couple of options.

First, I could make the argument that removing you from the only family you've known is unnecessary given you will be of age in a few months." He fluttered the cloth. "The courts are bogged down and might consider the case a waste of time. On the other hand, Bellinghamshire's powerful and might call in favors."

His kind always did. "How likely is the court to dismiss the case?"

He pinched the bridge of his nose and wagged his head back and forth. "I'd estimate we have about a fifty percent probability of winning, if you're willing to take the chance. That is, if the petition hasn't been approved already."

Fifty percent? Only one in two? Not odds she favored, by any means.

"What's the other possibility?" Brette ran her fingertips across the cloak's smooth velvet, the fabric strangely soothing, as was the repetitive motion.

"At this time, the inheritance is legally yours, so I could swiftly draft documentation assigning it in its entirety to a trustworthy person of your choice. As your acting guardian, Ravensdale can authorize the transaction. Once you come of age, the person you've selected can transfer everything back to you. Since I believe it's your money Bellinghamshire is after, he mightn't proceed with the guardianship claim."

Fingers still pressed to his nose, he closed his eyes as if deep in thought.

Much more appealing than the first suggestion. Mayhap he could do both?

"Except—" Mr. Shipwreck crumpled his mouth and opened his eyes.

What she saw there didn't encourage her.

Brette's anticipation plummeted off a cliff. "Except what?"

"Bellinghamshire could contest the procedure, though he's not likely to prevail unless he's already been assigned, or is close to being assigned, as your guardian. In which case, the transfer would be null and void."

Rot and bother.

What if the Chancery Court favored the duke?

Well, Brette wouldn't meekly pack her belongings and toddle to wherever the blazes her uncle lived. She'd vanish until her first-and-twentieth birthday. Eight months wasn't overly long.

Heath would help. Leventhorpe and Alex too.

Alex. How could she vanish and put him from her life?

One step at a time. It might not come to that. No sense getting ahead of yourself.

"It seems to me, Mr. Shipwreck, that the most critical thing at this point is discovering precisely how far the guardianship process has progressed." She'd better plan for the worst while hoping for the best.

He tucked several papers into a folder as he nodded. "Indeed. And I shall begin inquiring as soon as I've seen you home. Let's hope Lord Ravensdale is present, and I might have a word with him."

Two knocks announced Mr. Loomis again. He peered around the door. "Miss Culpepper, your coach has arrived."

Finally.

"Thank you, Loomis. I shall accompany Miss Culpepper. If Lord Ravensdale seeks her here, please tell him I've taken her home. And please inform her coachman I need a word with him." He placed his hat upon his head then draped a cloak across his arm before seizing his walking stick.

"Yes, sir." Bobbing his head, the secretary offered another apologetic smile. "Should I keep your intentions from anyone else who might inquire as to either of your whereabouts?"

Brette hadn't a doubt Mr. Loomis would go to his grave before revealing their plan.

"If Lord Wycombe should happen by, he may be apprised as well." Perhaps Alex would be home to receive the note. After tucking her handkerchief into her reticule, Brette swung her cape around her shoulders, secured the frogs, and gathered her other possessions.

Mr. Shipwreck lifted his cane a couple of inches. "It contains a short sword. Can't hurt to be prepared."

Against what, precisely?

A moment later, Mr. Loomis admitted Peters.

Hat in his hands, his attention shifted from Brette to Mr. Shipwreck. "My apologies for my tardiness, miss. After waiting in a lengthy line at the alchemist, a coach accident forced me to take a different route. The roads are getting slick too. I think it wise to depart at once."

"In a moment…Peters, is it?" Mr. Shipwreck raked his gaze over the burly coachman. "Miss Culpepper was followed here. Even now, we believe someone may lie in wait for her in the carriage parked across the street. I'll be riding with her, and I was curious if you carry a firearm."

Peters didn't flinch at the unusual requests. "I noticed the coach too. Thought it odd, sitting there on a day like this. The coachmen look miserable." His mouth tipped up. "And yes, I have a loaded pistol beneath my seat and a knife in my boot. His lordship insists upon it."

Thank goodness, Heath had had the foresight. Nevertheless, apprehension made Brette edgy. "We will flank Miss Culpepper as we exit. I'll have my secretary and clerk escort us as well. Drive directly home, taking the most public route, though it's slower. We want to be seen."

Peters bobbed his head. "A maid is in the carriage too, sir. She's a trifle—Flora upsets easily."

His consideration warmed Brette, and she'd make Heath aware.

"I don't think anyone would dare try anything. Nonetheless, we should be alert." For a solicitor, Mr. Shipwreck seemed uniquely prepared.

Moments later, hood covering her bonnet and surrounded by men, Brette descended the steps. No sooner had she left the building than the carriage across the street's door swung open, and a tall, dignified man emerged.

Not the Dowager Countess Wycombe, and given his first stare of fashion trappings, he wasn't anyone's lackey. He was, however, surprisingly surefooted considering the slushy ground. His elongated strides rapidly swallowed the between them. "Miss Culpepper?"

His drivers followed in his wake; huge chaps easily as strapping and intimidating as Peters. This didn't bode well.

"Don't speak, keep your head lowered, and get into the coach. Pull the shades too." Mr. Shipwreck basically heaved her into the interior a mere second before Peters slammed the door shut.

Mr. Shipwreck and his clerk placed themselves between the approaching man and the coach as she scrambled to yank the shades down.

Before she'd completely lowered the second one, the man grinned and flicked his wrist at them. "No need for this. I'm simply collecting my ward."

Dear God.

Bellinghamshire? Her uncle?

Flora, her eyes dinner-plate round, jerked the lap robes to her chin. Teeth chattering, she whispered, "Miss Brette, what's happening?"

"*Shh*, Flora. I'll explain later. I need to hear what being said outside." Brette pressed her ear near the freezing door. Blast, but the coach was cold within. A veritable ice box.

Peters didn't dare climb into the driver's seat in case Brette needed help staving off the three men, and neither could Mr. Shipwreck enter the carriage for fear of the men snatching her when he did.

She swallowed the bile rising to her throat, truly afraid for the first time in her life. What did her uncle intend to do with her? If the situation hadn't been so bloody frightening, she might've laughed at the absurdity of it.

"And who might you be?" Mr. Shipwreck

demanded, defiance in every starchy syllable. He didn't seem the least intimidated by the duke.

"Bellinghamshire." The duke's amiable tone hardened. "And the young woman in this coach is my niece and ward."

Done with pleasantries already?

Flora whimpered.

"*Shh*, it will be all right, Flora." Brette didn't know how.

"Ward? You are gravely mistaken, sir. Lord Ravensdale is her guardian," Mr. Shipwreck said.

Bellinghamshire laughed, a rather pleasant sound for such a vile man. "Not according to the Chancery Court, he isn't. I must insist you relinquish her to me before I have to take unpleasant measures or bring the authorities into it."

Muffled horses' hooves, along with springs squeaking and the whooshing of wheels turning, announced a vehicle's approach. Brette held her breath.

Let it be Heath or Alex.

Almost crying her frustration aloud when it rolled past, she pressed her forehead against the window.

Did Bellinghamshire truly think he could seize her outside her solicitor's office and haul her off, pell-mell? Surely he wasn't dimwitted enough to presume she'd go willingly?

Screeching and clawing and kicking? Yes.

Willingly? Never.

What an arrogant buffoon.

"I should welcome the authorities' intervention," Mr. Shipwreck boldly challenged. *Remember to double his fee.* "So unless you possess a writ proving you are whom you say you are, you will return to your conveyance and allow us to depart in peace." *Brilliant. A well- delivered blow.* "I'm certain you wouldn't want an attempted abduction linked to your name, Your Grace."

Oh, and another full-on facer. Well done you, Mr. Shipwreck.

She'd triple his fee. Indeed, she would.

A second coach's approach rang along the pavement, and before it lumbered to a halt, Heath's welcome, but angry voice rang out. "What goes on here?"

Her relief profound and fighting tears, Brette allowed herself a jubilant smile.

"Bellinghamshire, surprised you're about on a miserable day like this."

A joyous tear did leak from her eye. Dear Alex had come too.

"I thought you preferred the comforts of White's or Brooks's." A steely edge tempered Alex's geniality.

She tried to peek below the shade's folds, but only the thickly falling snowflakes and a row of men's backs met her inspection.

"Or a gaming hell, losing more funds," resonated a third droll voice. Leventhorpe? How was it possible he was here too?

Oh, you just try taking on this trio, Bellinghamshire.

Inhaling a bracing breath, Brette unlatched the door. She thrust it open, accidentally bumping Jacobson's back. He must have ridden back with Heath.

"I beg your pardon."

"Quite all right" His lips quirked, and he presented his hand to help her step down. "Which vehicle will you take, miss?"

"I don't know yet." Intentionally ignoring his grace, she cocked her head. Relation or not, they'd not been introduced. "Shall I ride with you, Ravensdale, or will you and the others join me?"

Everyone swung to face her.

She waved at Alex and Leventhorpe. "So wonderful to see you both."

More than wonderful. Marvelous. As was the flummoxed expression on her uncle's face.

Alex, his hands balled and the wrath of God accenting his angular cheeks, broke into a pleased smile.

She'd rather like him to punch her uncle.

"My dear niece, no sense in prolonging the inevitable. Do come along with me and meet your aunt and cousin." Bellinghamshire's mouth swept into an artificial smile, pleating the edges of his blueish-green eyes.

Her eyes.

Except a worldly toughness glinted in his.

He doesn't like me any more than I like him.

Brette leveled him her frostiest glance and angled her head. "Your Grace, do you normally conduct business in the midst of a snowstorm? I have an ill maid within this carriage, and rest assured, before I go anywhere with you, the team pulling this coach will sprout wings and fly."

Heath, Alex, and Leventhorpe chuckled.

"Reminds me of her cousin." A wicked smirk bent Leventhorpe's mouth.

"Her sister too," Heath agreed with an equally rakish grin. "Shall we?" He indicated Brette's carriage.

Something near a growl of fury escaped Bellinghamshire. "I have been awarded her guardianship, Ravensdale. It's merely a matter of receiving the documents from the court."

Heath lifted a shoulder an inch, and made to enter the carriage, Leventhorpe on his heels. "Well, until you have received them, she will remain with me."

Leventhorpe stepped into the coach and winked at Brette as he settled on the opposite seat. "Having yourself an adventure, are you?"

"Indeed. I've had quite the most remarkable morning." Had she ever. She raised the shades, and waved at Jacobson grinning at her from outside. He deserved a handsome tip. "Whatever are you doing in London, my lord?"

Leventhorpe waggled his auburn eyebrows. "Brooke wrote us and hinted you could use reinforcements."

She had?

Heath tossed a steely look over his shoulder as he entered the equipage. "Try to take Brette before you have proof of guardianship, Bellinghamshire, and I shall cut you down where you stand."

16

Something close to a sneer skewed Alex's mouth, and he raised a brow at the duke. His most you-unworthy-dog-go-lick-your-arse brow. Bellinghamshire possessed unsavory secrets he most definitely didn't want shared in the upper salons.

Alex folded his arms, asking softly, "Been to confession recently, Your Grace?"

Bellinghamshire blanched and suddenly found the pavement fascinating, but he didn't answer. He couldn't since Alex had been his rector and knew when the duke had last spilled his contemptuous guts.

Unworthy of Alex, especially given his previous position, but too satisfying to forego. After what Bellinghamshire had meant to do to Brette, his grace would receive no mercy.

A distinguished looking man—must be Shipwreck—a ruddy-cheeked red-headed youth, another fresh-faced youth, and a nervous, twitchy fellow keenly observed the exchange.

Alex pressed his advantage. "Seen Lord Dupresse of late? Heard he's seeking another young bride. What kind of a heartless, self-serving, despicable blackguard would force a woman to marry such a whoremonger?"

"Dupresse is after a wife again? Somebody's bloody desperate." Raven's incredulous question floated from the carriage, made louder by the snow-muffled outdoors.

"True," Leventhorpe acknowledged. "However, I want to know why Hawk thinks the problem critical enough to mention during the worst weather in years and when Bellinghamshire has stupidly threatened to make off with one of our own? One might suppose Hawk knows something more of the situation." The coach bounced lightly. "I shall find out."

Leventhorpe peered past the open doorway, such a look of feigned innocence on his face, Alex suppressed a snort. "I say, Wycombe, don't suppose you know the unfortunate bride's name?"

Silence, as heavy and dense as the falling snow, met his cheeky question.

"Me?" Brette's comprehending gasp made Alex

curl his fists. God would forgive him for laying Bellinghamshire out. Surely He would.

Smart chap, Leventhorpe. He'd deduced Bellinghamshire's intent too.

Alex gave a terse nod. "Oh, indeed, I do, and every fire in hell *will* freeze first."

Bellinghamshire's alarmed gaze flew to Alex's as a huge snowflake landed on the duke's nose.

Yes, white definitely tinged the lines bracketing his grace's mouth.

Bellinghamshire pounded the coach's side. "This isn't over, Ravensdale, but I'm not going to argue in public. My solicitor will be in touch."

He stomped to his carriage. Halfway there, he lost his footing and, arms flailing, skidded a few paces before landing on his arse. Cursing, he attempted to stand and fell again.

A feminine giggle rent the air.

Alex recognized the contagious laugh and grinned.

"Don't stand there, idiots. Help me up." His grace's drivers rushed to do his bidding as Alex made to join the others in the coach.

Two seats remained in the cramped conveyance. He could either shove himself onto the same bench as his two over-sized friends, or take the spot beside Brette.

Easy decision.

After quickly brushing snow from his shoulders, Alex climbed inside. As he slid onto the seat beside her, she offered him a sunny smile.

"I'm heartily glad to see you." Her gaze lit on each of the men in turn. "I confess, I was terrified."

"Me too," Flora volunteered. "I was afeared I'd swoon."

She sneezed and, seizing a well-used handkerchief, blew her nose. Brette patted the maid's hand. "It's all right now."

Shipwreck stuck his head into the door's opening. "The weather is too foul to stand here and go into detail, and I need to send my staff home. But suffice it to say, Miss Culpepper received the bulk of her grandfather's estate. He," the solicitor jerked his thumb in the direction of the carriage slowly pulling away from the curb, "doesn't own the clothes on his back. My advice? Find a safe place to hide her away until this is sorted out. Send me a note, and I'll meet you at Highfield Place House to discuss our options. Don't come here again."

With those words, he doffed his hat and made his way to his establishment, shooing his shivering staff before him.

"Hide me away?" Brette pulled a face. "Is that necessary?" Her countenance grew more troubled. "Alex, did you mean me? Has my uncle promised me to a ... a reprobate?"

A kind term for Dupresse.

"Fear not, Brette. It won't come to pass. I promise you." Alex took her hand, despite both Raven and Leventhorpe's raised brows. "Raven, I have an idea." Alex motioned to Leventhorpe. "Would you mind terribly escorting Flora to Highfield? I need to speak with Raven as Brette's guardian."

Too bad propriety forbade him asking Raven to leave too.

Leventhorpe's keen gaze assessed the snuffling, chaffed-nose maid. "Of course. I confess, I'm dying to know how Brette came to be Old Fusty Boot's heir, but I can wait to learn the whole of it."

Moments later, he and Flora, snuggly wrapped in a lap robe, climbed into the other coach and went on their way.

"First, I need to clarify something Shipwreck stated." Raven leaned forward, curiosity lighting his face. "You're the old duke's heir? How?"

"My parents married after all, and because my grandfather quarreled with his firstborn, he rewrote his will. It stipulated that the first legitimate offspring of either of his younger two sons was his heir." She lifted a shoulder an inch. "That's me."

Alex whistled. "I'll bet Bellinghamshire's beyond

furious."

"Desperate too, I'd say." Though casually spoken, Brette wasn't as relaxed as she pretended, and her gently curved mouth held no joy. "There's little chance he won't be named my guardian? Even though I'll be one-and-twenty in eight months?"

Raven shook his head, and rubbed his neck. "Bellinghamshire's your uncle. I'm merely your cousin's husband. Unfortunately, the sod has more of a legal claim than I do. That's why I left in such a rush this morning. A friend in the Chancery Court alerted me, and I spent the morning trying to determine how far the duke's claim has proceeded so I'd know what to do."

Alex crossed his arms and relaxed against the seat. "A husband would have a stronger claim."

"So what's your plan, Hawk? I suspect Bellinghamshire has gotten his way, and I'll shortly receive word Brette's been named his ward." Raven gave her a reassuring smile. "Hell *will* indeed freeze before I permit him to take you, my dear. Your sister would have my hide. If we have to, we'll leave England until you're of age."

Shivering and her teeth chattering—cold or nerves?—Brette hauled a robe onto her lap. "Thank you, Heath, but I fear you'll have no choice, and I can't allow Brooke to travel when she's expecting. Besides, your child should be born in England. I think I need to disappear for a spell. I won't tell anyone where I am until I come of age. The duke will have control of my fortune though."

"I have a better solution." Beneath the robe, Alex gathered her hand in his, and her encouraging smile made his heart trip over itself.

"Truly, Hawk? Now? You cannot wait at least until we reach Highfield?" Raven shook his head, reproach and empathy evident in his kind smile. "You need coaching on the matter, my dear fellow. A gentleman simply doesn't propose three times with an audience. It's most awkward for everyone."

Alex tucked Brette's hand close to his side. "This from a man who proposed *after* he won a woman's virtue in a wager and would've made her his mistress?"

"He has you there, Heath." Brette didn't seem the least perturbed that Alex intended to propose. "But before we go further, there's something I must ask you, Alex."

"Oh, my God." Raven's flabbergasted gaze bounced between them. "You're two of a kind. I should object, I suppose. But honestly, I can't think of one logical reason." He pointed at the blanket lying beside Brette. "Do you want me to cover my head with that robe and provide you a semblance of privacy?"

Could've obligingly ridden in the other coach.

Brette darted him a do-be-quiet glance before swallowing and meeting Alex's eyes. Her beatific mouth curving into a gentle smile, something akin to love glowing from the sea-green depths, she grasped both his hands.

Alex's lungs stalled. For certain she didn't mean to—

"Will you marry me, Alex? As soon as we can get a special license?"

Brette wanted to marry him. This woman who'd imprinted her smile, her essence on his soul wanted to be his wife. And the brave, daring darling asked him in front of her guardian.

"My dear, I'll be delighted to answer your question when we are alone. I was going to suggest we have a private moment when we get home." He gave Raven a quelling look. "I know you aren't the least romantic, but I am."

"Yes, so I've observed." Sarcasm thicker than molasses dripped from Raven's words.

In fact, Alex had arranged to have sweets and flowers delivered, and in his chambers an elegant ivory velvet box held an exquisite emerald-cut blue-green diamond, the likes of which he'd never before seen. He'd known the moment he spied the ring, rimmed with double rows of white diamonds, it must be Brette's.

The coach had barely skidded to a stop before Alex alighted. The day had grown twilight dark. Difficult to believe the clock had yet to strike one. He handed Brette down. "Will you meet me in the drawing room in thirty minutes?"

She gave him a saucy smile. "That long? How about fifteen? I just need to change into my slippers." With a little wave, she hurried ahead of him into the house.

As Alex and Raven ascended the stoop together, Alex gave Raven a sheepish grin. "I suppose I ought to formally ask for Brette's hand in marriage."

Raven slapped his shoulder as they stomped snow from their boots. "I believe we are way beyond that. If I refuse, I'll have the cousins wishing me ill. You have my blessing. She couldn't be marrying anyone finer. As soon as the weather clears, I'd be happy to acquire the special license. I don't think we dare wait."

"Well, as to that. I may have overstepped the bounds. Once my grandmother told me of Bellinghamshire's plans, I obtained a license before I returned home. A benefit of being a former cleric."

Raven stopped in his tracks. "Your grandmother told you? That's a story I need to hear."

Alex grinned. "She's coming around nicely.

Especially since I offered to let her live with Brette and me."

Raven's guffaw echoed off the entry walls and ceiling. "You are a saint, Hawk. A bloody saint."

A half an hour later, having collected the ring from his chamber and carefully displayed the flowers and sweets on the tea table, Alex checked the clock near his head for the sixth or seventh time.

One arm braced against the mantel, he stared into the fire, the flames, almost hypnotic. What delayed Brette?

She'd been the one to suggest fifteen minutes. Had she changed her mind?

Maybe this was too overwhelming, too rushed.

If she regretted her impetuous proposal and didn't come down, he'd forgive her. How could he not? His bruised heart wouldn't soon recover, though, and he closed his eyes, mouthing a silent prayer that something else delayed her. Nevertheless, her happiness mattered above everything, and no matter what the future held, whether their paths intertwined or separated, Brette would forever be branded upon his spirit and heart.

"Alex?"

Slowly, hesitant to face her, to hear what she might say, he raised his head.

A vision of loveliness stood silhouetted in the

doorway, and his breathing stalled. She'd changed into a stunning periwinkle gown. A delicate blue rose garland encircled her hair, and dainty earrings hung from her shell-like ears.

"I'm sorry I'm late. I decided to change." After closing the door, she floated further into the room.

Surly a positive sign. No chaperone and a firmly closed door He held his arms wide. "Come here."

She flew into his embrace, where she was meant to be, the sweetest of homecomings. In his arms, for eternity.

He tilted her chin, and she closed her eyes. Their lips met in a kiss penetrating his inner-most being, fusing her soul with his. From the first moment he'd seen her, his spirit had recognized its mate.

Nuzzling her neck, relishing her little passionate sighs and gasps, he teased her. "So, minx, do you want my answer?"

She laughed and pointed at the crimson roses and sweetmeat assortment. "There's my answer, I think."

"No, not entirely." Alex removed the ring from his little finger and folded to one knee.

Holding one of her hands in his, he slipped the diamond onto her finger.

Holding up her hand, she admired the jewel. "It's utterly breathtaking. Thank you."

"Let me finish, darling, else I muck this up and ruin the moment." He drew in a deep breath.

Ought to have rehearsed this part more, but he'd give it a go, nevertheless.

"Brette Anastasia Wiliminia Culpepper, will you grant me a lifetime of overwhelming joy, happiness I don't deserve—yet covet with my whole heart—and agree to take this humble, flawed man who loves you more than he loves his own life as your husband?"

She cupped his cheek, giving him a tender smile. "Are you going poetic on me, Alex? The effects of having been a cleric or a would-be actor?"

"Is it working?" Weren't women supposed to get teary-eyed and say yes straightaway? Not tease and ask cheeky questions?

Brette kneeled before him and, cradling his face, pressed her soft, sweet mouth to his. "I never needed anything but to know you love me as much as I adore you. And that was why you wanted to marry me, not because you felt obligated. I've loved you since you descended from the carriage at Esherton Green, and I couldn't tear my eyes from you. I intended to tell you that last night."

"Ah, and I assumed you invited me to your bed."

"Well, I was, rather, in a roundabout way." Her throaty chuckle, more of a tantalizing purr, had him reconsidering his scruples.

Alex helped her stand then gathered her tempting form into his embrace. Contentment flooded him, warm and secure. He could remain like this for eternity. "Believe me, I've never wanted anything more, except to make you my wife, which I was determined to do before accepting so irresistible an invitation."

Cheeks rosy, Brette murmured, "My intentions went astray."

"You haven't answered my question, darling." He nipped her lower lip. Could a clergyman be persuaded to perform the ceremony this afternoon?

"How's this for an answer?" She stood on her toes, wrapped her slender arms about his neck, and kissed him with such tender reverence that tears stung behind his eyes. "Will that answer do, my dearest love?"

He swallowed and squeezed her tight. "That'll do. Indeed. That'll do."

The most powerful intention
is no match for unconditional love.
*~Appearances and Attitude—The Genteel Lady's
Guide to Practical Living*

Epilogue

January 1823 High Wycombe

Brette slipped her wrap off, and after tossing it on the armchair beside the window, slid into bed. Even with the hearty fire, a slight chill lingered in the chamber. Alex would have her warm soon enough though.

He promptly hauled her into his strong embrace, and she snuggled against his solid chest, the soft, golden hairs tickling her nose. "*Brrr.* It's snowing again. Our company may be here a while longer than expected."

Dropping a kiss on her nose, he towed the bedcovering over her shoulders. "I'd better keep you warm then, Lady Wycombe, and I enjoy having your family. They get along famously with Grandmama and are most forgiving of her tetchy moments."

"They are, aren't they? We didn't know our grandparents. I think Brooke and Blythe have adopted Grandmama as theirs. I'm sure Blaike and Blaire will too when they meet her. Besides, she's rarely peevish now. Love and acceptance have changed her, softened her ragged edges."

"They have indeed," he murmured into her hair.

They'd transformed her too. The remarkable man lying beside her had carved a niche in her heart and taken up permanent residence there.

"Be warned though, my darling wife. I've detected her eyeing Brooke's belly before turning her matriarch's eye on me. She's expecting an announcement soon."

"In due time." Blythe also increased, and Brette expected she'd soon be in the family way as well. Until then, she coveted this time with Alex. Breathing in his manly scent, she permitted a small upward tilt of her mouth. She wouldn't tire of his smell. Or him. He'd introduced her to passion exceeding her dreams and a love she'd believed beyond her.

He rested his chin atop her head, his breath warming her scalp. "Happy, love?"

"Deliriously so." They'd been married two months, and each day brought her greater joy. "Are you? I don't mean us, but in general? You readily admit you weren't cut from a cleric cloth—"

Alex chuckled, while drawing lazy circles on her bare shoulder, causing shivers of pleasure. "I'll say I wasn't. I'm sure the Lord will have much to say to me on judgement day. Mr. Dalton's a far better fit than I ever was."

"You're too hard on yourself, Alex. You did your best. That's all anyone's able to do, especially when forced into circumstances not of our choosing. But the earldom— You didn't covet a title either."

"I didn't expect to inherit, and I failed to contemplate the enormity of the position." His exploration gravitated lower, and he caressed her hip, pulling her nightgown up until he met bare skin. "In many ways, it's much like being a rector—the care and responsibility and the wellbeing of others fell to me. I can only hope I'm a better earl than my cousin was."

Tracing his bristly jaw with her forefinger, enjoying the whiskers abrading her skin, she kissed his neck. "There's no doubt of that, darling. If he hadn't tupped the footman's sister, gotten her with child, and the poor thing hadn't died during childbirth, her grief-mad brother wouldn't have set the fire. It doesn't excuse his revenge, but I'm sure he felt utterly powerless against a peer."

"I give you my word, I won't abuse my title. I'd much prefer to use the power accompanying the earldom to help the less fortunate. I guess a portion of my former life will always remain with me."

She raised her head and sought his eyes. "I know you won't, Alex. You're not like your cousin or my uncle." A muffled giggle escaped her. "I can't help but laugh when I recall Bellinghamshire's expression when he stalked into the drawing room a week after our ugly encounter. There we were. Me on your lap, and your hand..."

Alex's chest shook with mirth. "A gentleman catching his niece in a compromising position ought to have demanded I marry you instead of victoriously waving court documents and telling you to pack your belongings."

"And when you told him my leaving would ruin our wedding trip—" Laughter bubbled up her throat, and several seconds passed before she composed herself. "I don't think I've ever observed a grown man more confounded."

"Almost as enjoyable as the Gambwells' reactions in Hyde Park the next day." He kissed her nose. "Most wicked of me, I confess. I'm not sure whether our marriage or your change in status befuddled them more."

"The world is full of kind, decent people, and I refuse to let the others steal my joy ever again." Brette touched his nipple, grinning when he shuddered. She liked this power over him.

"Well said, my love." Alex's exploration grew bolder, and familiar sensations awakened. She'd acquiesce in a bit. She wanted to savor this moment, commit it to memory.

Shifting, Brette rested in the groove between his shoulder and chest and scrutinized the canopy overhead. Dust in the pleats? Years of neglect contributed to High Wycombe's private chambers being in sore need of repair and refurbishing.

At first, Alex had argued against Brette using her inheritance to improve and restore the manor, but when she reminded him she was his helpmate, he'd conceded. He'd also readily agreed to a trust for Genevia; one her parents couldn't borrow a shilling from.

Brette gripped his hairy thigh. "Alex, I nearly forgot. I received a letter from Mr. Shipwreck today. He's found a property he thinks perfect for our charity school." She tilted her head to look at him. "I'd like us to tour it as soon as possible. He doesn't think it will remain available for long."

Alex angled his chin upward before resuming his sensual assault. "When the weather clears again, we can journey to London. Any luck with a location for the women's college?"

She suppressed a gasp when he boldly cupped a breast. He was certainly determined to seduce her tonight. His methods were proving most effective. She could barely gather her thoughts.

What had he asked? Oh, yes. The college.

"Nothing yet. I think I may wait until Blaire and Blaike return and ask what their opinions are. Based on their experiences, they may have useful tips, and between the foundling hospital and the charity school, I'm sure I'll be kept busy."

"Don't forget attending to your wifely duties." He squeezed her bottom and rocked his pelvis into her thigh, his arousal evident.

"*Tsk.* Duties are something one's obliged to do." She palmed his heavy, silken flesh, earning a gasp of pleasure. "This, dear husband, is a morsel of heaven on earth."

USA Today Bestselling, award-winning author COLLETTE CAMERON® scribbles Scottish and Regency historicals featuring dashing rogues and scoundrels and the intrepid damsels who re-form them. Blessed with an overactive and witty muse that won't stop whispering new romantic romps in her ear, she's lived in Oregon her entire life, though she dreams of living in Scotland part-time. A self-confessed Cadbury chocoholic, you'll always find a dash of inspiration and a pinch of humor in her sweet-to-spicy timeless romances®.

Explore **Collette's worlds** at
www.collettecameron.com!

Join her **VIP Reader Club** and **FREE newsletter**.
Giggles guaranteed!

FREE BOOK: Join Collette's The Regency Rose®
VIP Reader Club to get updates on book releases, cover
reveals, contests and giveaways she reserves
exclusively for email and newsletter followers. Also,
any deals, sales, or special promotions are offered to
club members first. She will not share your name or
email, nor will she spam you.

http://bit.ly/TheRegencyRoseGift

Dearest Reader,

I knew from the moment Brette Culpepper met Vicar Alexander Hawksworth in **The Earl and the Spinster** and she thought he was a valet, that those two needed their own romance.

Though **The Lord and the Wallflower** is a tad more somber in parts than the two previous books in the series, there are threads of humor and the devotion the Culpepper misses have for each other doesn't wane a jot.

Brette turned out to be a much more complex character than I'd first imagined, and Alex... Well, you've read the novel and uncovered his secrets!

I'm delighted you chose to read Brette and Alex's story, and I hope you enjoyed their tale enough to explore the other books in The Culpepper Misses series as well as some of my other historical romance novels.

Please consider telling other readers why you enjoyed this book by reviewing it. Not only do I truly want to hear your thoughts, reviews are crucial for an author to succeed. **Even if you only leave a line or two, I'd very much appreciate it.**

So, with that I'll leave you.

Here's wishing you many happy hours of reading, more happily ever afters than you can possibly enjoy in a lifetime, and abundant blessings to you and your loved-ones.

The Earl and the Spinster

The Culpepper Misses, Book One

Would you sacrifice everything save your family?
Even your virtue?

Caution: This book contains one stern lord with a dark secret he wants kept at all cost, a beautiful spinster smarter than the average man, an endearing, portly Welsh Corgi known to pee on gentlemen's boots, and a passel of well-meaning sisters and cousins who find themselves in one conundrum after the other.

Brooke Culpepper resigned herself to spinsterhood when she turned down the only marriage proposal she'd likely ever receive to care for her sister and cousins. After her father dies, a distant cousin inherits the estate, becoming their guardian, but he permits Brooke to act in his stead.

Heath, Earl of Ravensdale detests the countryside and is

none too pleased to discover five young women call the dairy farm he won, and intends to sell, their home.

Desperate, pauper poor, and with nowhere to go, Brooke proposes a wager. Heath's stakes? The farm. Hers? Her virtue. The land holds no interest for Heath, but Brooke definitely does, and he accepts her challenge. Will they both live to regret their impulsiveness?

Excerpt

Enjoy the first chapter of

The Earl and the Spinster

The Culpepper Misses, Book One

Even when most prudently considered,
and with the noblest of intentions, one who
wagers with chance oft finds oneself empty-handed.
~Wisdom and Advice—The Genteel Lady's
Guide to Practical Living

Esherton Green,
Near Acton, Cheshire, England
Early April 1822

*W**as I born under an evil star or cursed from my first breath?*

Brooke Culpepper suppressed the urge to shake her fist at the heavens and berate The Almighty aloud. The devil boasted better luck than she. My God, now two *more* cows struggled to regain their strength?

She slid Richard Mabry, Esherton Green's steward-turned-overseer, a worried glance from beneath her lashes as she chewed her lower lip and paced before the unsatisfactory fire in the study's hearth. The soothing aroma of wood smoke, combined with linseed oil, old leather, and the faintest trace of Papa's pipe tobacco, bathed the room. The scents reminded her of happier times but did little to calm her frayed nerves.

Sensible gray woolen skirts swishing about her ankles, she whirled to make the return trip across the once-bright green and gold Axminster carpet, now so threadbare, the oak floor peeked through in numerous places. Her scuffed half-boots fared little better, and she hid a wince when the scrap of leather she'd used to cover the hole in her left sole this morning slipped loose again.

From his comfortable spot in a worn and faded wingback chair, Freddy, her aged Welsh corgi, observed her progress with soulful brown eyes, his muzzle propped on stubby paws. Two ancient tabbies lay curled so tightly together on the cracked leather sofa that determining where one ended and the other began was difficult.

What was she to do? Brooke clamped her lip harder

and winced.

Should she venture to the barn to see the cows herself?

What good would that do? She knew little of doctoring cattle and so left the animals' care in Mr. Mabry's capable hands. Her strength lay in the financial administration of the dairy farm and her ability to stretch a shilling as thin as gossamer.

She cast a glance at the bay window and, despite the fire, rubbed her arms against the chill creeping along her spine. A frenzied wind whipped the lilac branches and scraped the rain-splattered panes. The tempest threatening since dawn had finally unleashed its full fury, and the fierce winds battering the house gave the day a peculiar, eerie feeling—as if portending something ominous.

At least Mabry and the other hands had managed to get the cattle tucked away before the gale hit. The herd of fifty—no, sixty, counting the newborn calves— chewed their cud and weathered the storm inside the old, but sturdy, barns.

As she peered through the blurry pane, a shingle ripped loose from the farthest outbuilding—a retired stone dovecote. After the wind tossed the slat around for a few moments, the wood twirled to the ground, where it flipped end over end before wedging beneath a gangly shrub. Two more shingles hurled to the earth, this time from one of the barns.

Flimflam and goose-butt feathers.

Brooke tamped down a heavy sigh. Each structure on the estate, including the house, needed some sort of repair or replacement: roofs, shutters, stalls, floors, stairs, doors, siding...dozens of items required fixing, and she could seldom muster the funds to go about it properly.

"Another pair of cows struggling, you say, Mr. Mabry?"

Concern etched on his weathered features, Mabry wiped rain droplets from his face as water pooled at his muddy feet.

"Yes, Miss Brooke. The four calves born this mornin' fare well, but two of the cows, one a first-calf heifer, aren't standin' yet. And there's one weak from birthin' her calf yesterday." His troubled gaze strayed to the window. "Two more ladies are in labor. I best return to the barn. They seemed fine when I left, but I'd as soon be nearby."

Brooke nodded once. "Yes, we mustn't take any chances."

The herd had already been reduced to a minimum by disease and sales to make ends meet. She needed every shilling the cows' milk brought. Losing another, let alone two or three good breeders...

No, I won't think of it.

She stopped pacing and forced a cheerful smile. Nonetheless, from the skeptical look Mabry speedily masked, his thoughts ran parallel to hers—one reason she put her trust in the man. Honest and intelligent, he'd worked alongside her to restore the beleaguered herd and farm after Papa died. Their existence, their livelihood, everyone at Esherton's future depended on the estate flourishing once more.

"It's only been a few hours." *Almost nine, truth to tell.* Brooke scratched her temple. "Perhaps the ladies need a little more time to recover." *If they recovered.* "The calves are strong, aren't they?" *Please, God, they must be.* She held her breath, anticipating Mabry's response.

His countenance lightened and the merry sparkle returned to his eyes. "Aye, the mites are fine. Feedin' like they're hollow to their wee hooves."

Tension lessoned its ruthless grip, and hope peeked from beneath her vast mound of worries.

Six calves had been guaranteed in trade to her neighbor and fellow dairy farmer, Silas Huffington, for the grain and medicines he'd provided to see Esherton Green's herd through last winter. Brooke didn't have the means to pay him if the calves didn't survive—though the old reprobate had hinted he'd make her a deal of a much less respectable nature if she ran short of cattle with which to barter. Each pence she'd stashed away—groat by miserable groat, these past four years—lay in the hidden drawer of Papa's desk and must go to purchase a bull.

Wisdom had decreed replacing Old Buford two years ago but, short on funds, she'd waited until it was too late. His heart had stopped while he performed the duties expected of a breeding bull. Not the worst way to cock up one's toes...er, hooves, but she'd counted on him siring at least two-score calves this season and wagered everything on the calving this year and next. The poor brute had expired before he'd completed the job.

Her thoughts careened around inside her skull. Without a bull, she would lose everything.

My home, care of my sister and cousins, my reasons for existing.

She squared her shoulders, resolution strengthening her. She still retained the Culpepper sapphire parure set. If all else failed, she would pawn the jewelry. She'd planned on using the money from the gems' sale to bestow small marriage settlements on the girls. Still, pawning the set was a price worth paying to keep her family at Esherton Green, even if it meant that any chance of her sister and three cousins securing a decent match would evaporate faster than a dab of milk on a hot cook stove. Good standing and breeding meant little if one's fortune proved meaner than a churchyard beggar's.

"How's the big bull calf that came breech on Sunday?" Brooke tossed the question over her shoulder as she poked the fire and encouraged the blaze to burn hotter. After setting the tool aside, she faced the overseer.

"Greediest of the lot." Mabry laughed and slapped his thigh. "Quite the appetite he has, and friendly as our Freddy there. Likes his ears scratched too."

Brooke chuckled and ran her hand across Freddy's spine. The dog wiggled in excitement and stuck his rear legs straight out behind him, gazing at her in adoration. In his youth, he'd been an excellent cattle herder. Now he'd gone fat and arthritic, his sweet face gray to his eyebrows. On occasion, he still dashed after the cattle, the instinctive drive to herd deep in the marrow of his bones.

Another shudder shook her. Why was she so blasted cold today? She relented and placed a good-sized log atop the others. The feeble flames hissed and spat before greedily engulfing the new addition. Lord, she prayed she wasn't ailing. She simply couldn't afford to become ill.

A scratching at the door barely preceded the entrance of Duffen bearing a tea service. "Gotten to where a man cannot find a quiet corner to shut his eyes for a blink or two anymore."

Shuffling into the room, he yawned and revealed how few teeth remained in his mouth. One sock sagged around his ankle, his grizzled hair poked every which way, and his shirttail hung askew. Typical Duffen.

"Devil's day, it is." He scowled in the window's direction, his mouth pressed into a grim line. "Mark my words, trouble's afoot."

Not quite a butler, but certainly more than a simple retainer, the man, now hunched from age, had been a fixture at Esherton Green Brooke's entire life. He loved the place as much as, if not more than, she, and she couldn't afford to hire a servant to replace him. A light purse had forced Brooke to let the household staff go when Papa died. The cook, Mrs. Jennings, Duffen, and Flora, a maid-of-all-work, had stayed on. However, they received no salaries—only room and board.

The income from the dairy scarcely permitted Brooke to retain a few milkmaids and stable hands, yet not once had she heard a whispered complaint from anyone.

Everybody, including Brooke, her sister, Brette,

and their cousins—Blythe, and the twins, Blaike and Blaire—did their part to keep the farm operating at a profit. A meager profit, particularly as, for the past five years, Esherton Green's legal heir, Sheridan Gainsborough, had received half the proceeds. In return, he permitted Brooke and the girls to reside there. He'd also been appointed their guardian. But, from his silence and failure to visit the farm, he seemed perfectly content to let her carry on as provider and caretaker.

"Ridiculous law. Only the next male in line can inherit," she muttered.

Especially when he proved a disinterested bore. Papa had thought so too, but the choice hadn't been his to make. If only she could keep the funds she sent to Sheridan each quarter, Brooke could make something of Esherton and secure her sister and cousins' futures too.

If wishes were gold pieces, I'd be rich indeed.

Brooke sneezed then sneezed again. Dash it all. A cold?

The fresh log snapped loudly, and Brooke started. The blaze's heat had failed to warm her opinion of her second cousin. She hadn't met him and lacked a personal notion of his character, but Papa had hinted that Sheridan was a scallywag and possessed unsavory habits.

A greedy sot, too.

The one time her quarterly remittance had been late, because Brooke had taken a tumble and broken her arm, he'd written a disagreeable letter demanding his money.

His money, indeed.

Sheridan had threatened to sell Esherton Green's acreage and turn her and the foursome onto the street if she ever delayed payment again.

A ruckus beyond the entrance announced the girls' arrival. Laughing and chatting, the blond quartet billowed into the room. Their gowns, several seasons out of fashion, in no way detracted from their charm, and pride swelled in Brooke's heart. Lovely, both in countenance and disposition, and the dears worked hard too.

"Duffen says we're to have tea in here today." Attired in a Pomona green gown too short for her tall frame, Blaike plopped on to the sofa. Her twin, Blaire, wearing a similar dress in dark rose and equally inadequate in length, flopped beside her.

Each girl scooped a drowsy cat into her lap. The cats' wiry whiskers twitched, and they blinked their sleepy amber eyes a few times before closing them once more as the low rumble of contented purrs filled the room.

"Yes, I didn't think we needed to light a fire in the

drawing room when this one will suffice." As things stood, too little coal and seasoned firewood remained to see them comfortably until summer.

Brette sailed across the study, her slate-blue gingham dress the only one of the quartet's fashionably long enough. Repeated laundering had turned the garment a peculiar greenish color, much like tarnished copper. She looped her arm through Brooke's.

"Look, dearest." Brette pointed to the tray. "I splurged and made a half-batch of shortbread biscuits. It's been so long since we've indulged, and today is your birthday. To celebrate, I insisted on fresh tea leaves as well."

Brooke would have preferred to ignore the day.

Three and twenty.

On the shelf. Past her prime. Long in the tooth. Spinster. *Old maid.*

She'd relinquished her one chance at love. In order to nurse her ailing father and assume the care of her young sister and three orphaned cousins, she'd refused Humphrey Benbridge's proposal. She couldn't have put her happiness before their welfare and deserted them when they needed her most. Who would've cared for them if she hadn't?

No one.

Mr. Benbridge controlled the purse strings, and

Humphrey had neither offered nor been in a position to take on their care. Devastated, or so he'd claimed, he'd departed to the continent five years ago.

She'd not seen him since.

Nonetheless, his sister, Josephina, remained a friend and occasionally remarked on Humphrey's travels abroad. Burying the pieces of her broken heart beneath hard work and devotion to her family, Brooke had rolled up her sleeves and plunged into her forced role as breadwinner, determined that sacrificing her love not be in vain.

Yes, it grieved her that she wouldn't experience a man's passion or bear children, but to wallow in doldrums was a waste of energy and emotion. Instead, she focused on building a future for her sister and cousins—so they might have what she never would— and allowed her dreams to fade into obscurity.

"Happy birthday." Brette squeezed her hand.

Brooke offered her sister a rueful half-smile. "Ah, I'd hoped you'd forgotten."

"Don't be silly, Brooke. We couldn't forget your special day." Twenty-year-old Blythe—standing with her hands behind her—grinned and pulled a small, neatly-wrapped gift tied with a cheerful yellow ribbon from behind her. Sweet dear. She'd used the trimming from her gown to adorn the package.

"Hmph. Need seedcake an' champagne to celebrate a birthday properly." The contents of the tray rattled and clanked when Duffen scuffed his way to the table between the sofa and chairs. After depositing the tea service, he lifted a letter from the surface. Tea dripped from one stained corner. "This arrived for you yesterday, Miss Brooke. I forgot where I'd put it until just now."

If I can read it with the ink running to London and back.

He shook the letter, oblivious to the tawny droplets spraying every which way.

Mabry raised a bushy gray eyebrow, and the twins hid giggles by concealing their faces in the cat's striped coats.

Brette set about pouring the tea, although her lips twitched suspiciously.

Freddy sat on his haunches and barked, his button eyes fixed on the paper, evidently mistaking it for a tasty morsel he would've liked to sample. He licked his chops, a testament to his waning eyesight.

"Thank you, Duffen." Brooke took the letter by one soggy corner. Holding it gingerly, she flipped it over. No return address.

"Aren't you going to read it?" Blythe set the gift on the table before settling on the sofa and smoothing her skirt. They didn't get a whole lot of post at Esherton. Truth be known, this was the first letter in months. Blythe's gaze roved to the other girls and the equally eager expressions on their faces. "We're on pins and needles," she quipped, fluttering her hands and winking.

Brooke smiled and cracked the brownish wax seal with her fingernail. Their lives had become rather monotonous, so much so that a simple, *soggy*, correspondence sent the girls into a dither of anticipation.

My Dearest Cousin...

Brooke glanced up. "It's from Sheridan.

The Marquis and the Vixen

The Culpepper Misses, Book Two

Is protecting his honor more important than winning her heart?

Caution: This book contains a nobleman with a dark past, a strong-minded miss who is willing to cause a scandal if it means she can leave London, a spoiled, aging Welsh Corgi with digestive disruptions that can clear a room, and an entourage of goodhearted sisters and cousins whose antics land them in conundrum after conundrum.

Intrepid and outspoken…

Dragged to London for a Season, Blythe Culpepper is dismayed to learn her guardian has enlisted the devilishly attractive Lord Leventhorpe—the one man she detests—to assist with her Come Out. Since their first encounter, hostile looks and cutting retorts have abounded whenever they meet. Still, she cannot deny the way her body reacts when he's near. So perhaps it's no surprise that upon overhearing another woman scheming to entrap Tristan into marriage, Blythe risks all to warn him.

Haunted by childhood trauma…

Tristan, the austere and controlled Marquis of Leventhorpe, usually avoids social gatherings. So why, against his better judgement, does he agree to aid his closest friend in presenting the Culpeppers to the ton? Might it be because one particular Culpepper stirs more than his interest? Blythe taxes him to his limits with her sharp wit and even sharper tongue. Yet, he cannot deny the beauty fascinates him.

However, when a past enemy comes calling, using Blythe to settle old scores, Tristan must decide if protecting his honor is more important than winning the heart of the woman he has come to love.

A Kiss for Miss Kingsley

The Honorable Rogues®, Book One

Formerly titled *A Kiss for Miss Kingsley*

A lonely wallflower. A future viscount.
A second chance at love.

Olivia Kingsley didn't expect to be swept off her feet and receive a marriage proposal two weeks into her first Season. However, one delicious dance with Allen Wimpleton, and her future is sealed. Or so she thinks until her eccentric father suddenly announces he's moving the family to the Caribbean for a year.

Terrified of losing Olivia, Allen begs her to elope, but she refuses. Distraught at her leaving, and unaware of her father's ill-health, Allen doubts her love and foolishly demands she choose—him or her father.

Heartbroken at his callousness, Olivia turns her back on

their love. The year becomes three, enough time for her broken heart to heal, and after her father dies, she returns to England.

Coming face to face with Allen at a ball, she realizes she never purged him from her heart.

But can they overcome their pasts and old wounds to trust love again? Or has Allen found another in her absence?

Enjoy the first chapter of
A Kiss for a Rogue
The Honorable Rogues®, Book One

A lady must never forget
her manners nor lose her composure.
~A Lady's Guide to Proper Comportment

London, England
Late May, 1818

"**T**his is a monumental mistake."

God's toenails. What were you thinking, Olivia Kingsley, agreeing to Auntie Muriel's addlepated scheme?

Why had she ever agreed to this farce?

Fingering the heavy ruby pendant hanging at the

hollow of her neck, Olivia peeked out the window as the conveyance rounded the corner onto Berkeley Square. Good God. Carriage upon carriage, like great shiny beetles, lined the street beside an ostentatious manor. Her heart skipped a long beat, and she ducked out of sight.

Braving another glance from the window's corner, her stomach pitched worse than a ship amid a hurricane. The full moon's milky light, along with the mansion's rows of glowing diamond-shaped panes, illuminated the street. Dignified guests in their evening finery swarmed before the grand entrance and on the granite stairs as they waited their turn to enter Viscount and Viscountess Wimpleton's home.

The manor had acquired a new coat of paint since she had seen it last. She didn't care for the pale lead shade, preferring the previous color, a pleasant, welcoming bronze green. Why anyone living in Town would choose to wrap their home in such a chilly color was beyond her. With its enshrouding fog and perpetually overcast skies, London boasted every shade of gray already.

Three years in the tropics, surrounded by vibrant

flowers, pristine powdery beaches, a turquoise sea, and balmy temperatures had rather spoiled her against London's grime and stench. How long before she grew accustomed to the dank again? The gloom? The smell?

Never.

Shivering, Olivia pulled her silk wrap snugger. Though late May, she'd been nigh on to freezing since the ship docked last week.

A few curious guests turned to peer in their carriage's direction. A lady swathed in gold silk and dripping diamonds, spoke into her companion's ear and pointed at the gleaming carriage. Did she suspect someone other than Aunt Muriel sat behind the distinctive Daventry crest?

Trepidation dried Olivia's mouth and tightened her chest. Would many of the *ton* remember her?

Stupid question, that. Of course she would be remembered.

Much like ivy—its vines clinging tenaciously to a tree—or a barnacle cemented to a rock, one couldn't easily be pried from the upper ten thousand's memory. But, more on point, would anyone recall her fascination with Allen Wimpleton?

Inevitably.

Coldness didn't cause the new shudder rippling from her shoulder to her waist.

Yes. Attending the ball was a featherbrained solicitation for disaster. No good could come of it. Flattening against the sky-blue and gold-trimmed velvet squab in the corner of her aunt's coach, Olivia vehemently shook her head.

"I cannot do it. I thought I could, but I positively cannot."

A curl came loose, plopping onto her forehead.

Bother.

The dratted, rebellious nuisance that passed for her hair escaped its confines more often than not. She shoved the annoying tendril beneath a pin, having no doubt the tress would work its way free again before evenings end. Patting the circlet of rubies adorning her hair, she assured herself the band remained secure. The treasure had belonged to Aunt Muriel's mother, a Prussian princess, and no harm must come to it.

Olivia's pulse beat an irregular staccato as she searched for a plausible excuse for refusing to attend the ball after all. She wouldn't lie outright, which ruled out her initial impulse to claim a *megrim*.

"I ... we—" She wiggled her white-gloved fingers at her brother, lounging on the opposite seat. "Were not invited."

Contented as their fat cat, Socrates, after lapping a saucer of fresh cream, Bradford settled his laughing gaze on her. "Yes, we mustn't do anything untoward."

Terribly vulgar, that. Arriving at a *haut ton* function, no invitation in hand. She and Bradford mightn't make it past the vigilant majordomo, and then what were they to do? Scuttle away like unwanted pests? Mortifying and prime tinder for the gossips.

"Whatever will people *think*?" Bradford thrived on upending Society. If permitted, he would dance naked as a robin just to see the reactions. He cocked a cinder-black brow, his gray-blue eyes holding a challenge.

Toad.

Olivia yearned to tell him to stop giving her that loftier look. Instead, she bit her tongue to keep from sticking it out at him like she had as a child. Irrationality warred with reason, until her common sense finally prevailed. "I wouldn't want to impose, is all I meant."

"Nonsense, darling. It's perfectly acceptable for

you and Bradford to accompany me." The seat creaked as Aunt Muriel, the Duchess of Daventry, bent forward to scrutinize the crowd. She patted Olivia's knee. "Lady Wimpleton is one of my dearest friends. Why, we had our come-out together, and I'm positive had she known that you and Bradford had recently returned to England, she would have extended an invitation herself."

Olivia pursed her lips.

Not if she knew the volatile way her son and I parted company, she wouldn't have.

A powerful peeress, few risked offending Aunt Muriel, and she knew it well. She could haul a haberdasher or a milkmaid to the ball and everyone would paste artificial smiles on their faces and bid the duo a pleasant welcome. Reversely, if someone earned her scorn, they had best pack-up and leave London permanently before doors began slamming in their faces. Her influence rivaled that of the Almack's patronesses.

Bradford shifted, presenting Olivia with his striking profile as he, too, took in the hubbub before the manor. "You will never be at peace—never be able to move on—unless you do this."

That morsel of knowledge hadn't escaped her, which was why she had agreed to the scheme to begin with. Nevertheless, that didn't make seeing Allen Wimpleton again any less nerve-wracking.

"You must go in, Livy," Bradford urged, his countenance now entirely brotherly concern.

She stopped plucking at her mantle and frowned. "Please don't call me that, Brady."

Once, a lifetime ago, Allen had affectionately called her Livy—until she had refused to succumb to his begging and run away to Scotland. Regret momentarily altered her heart rhythm.

Bradford hunched one of his broad shoulders and scratched his eyebrow. "What harm can come of it? We'll only stay as long as you like, and I promise, I shall remain by your side the entire time."

Their aunt's unladylike snort echoed throughout the carriage.

"And the moon only shines in the summer." Her voice dry as desert sand, and skepticism peaking her eyebrows high on her forehead, Aunt Muriel fussed with her gloves. "Nephew, I have never known you to forsake an opportunity to become, er ..."

She slid Olivia a guarded glance. "Shall we say, become better acquainted with the ladies? This Season, there are several tempting beauties and a particularly large assortment of amiable young widows eager for a *distraction*."

Did Aunt Muriel truly believe Olivia don't know about Bradford's reputation with females? She was neither blind nor ignorant.

He turned and flashed their aunt one of his dazzling smiles, his deeply tanned face making it all the more brighter. "All pale in comparison to you two lovelies, no doubt."

Olivia made an impolite noise and, shaking her head, aimed her eyes heavenward in disbelief.

Doing it much too brown. Again.

Bradford was too charming by far—one reason the fairer sex were drawn to him like ants to molasses. She'd been just as doe-eyed and vulnerable when it came to Allen.

"Tish tosh, young scamp. Your compliments are wasted on me." Still, Aunt Muriel slanted her head, a pleased smile hovered on her lightly-painted mouth and pleating the corners of her eyes. "Besides, if you attach yourself to your sister, she won't have an opportunity to find herself alone with young Wimpleton."

Olivia managed to keep her jaw from unhinging as she gaped at her aunt. She snapped her slack mouth shut with an audible click. "Shouldn't you be cautioning me *not* to be alone with a gentleman?"

Aunt Muriel chuckled and patted Olivia's knee again. "That rather defeats the purpose in coming tonight then, doesn't it, dear?" Giving a naughty wink, she nudged Olivia. "I do hope Wimpleton kisses you. He's such a handsome young man. Quite the Corinthian too."

A hearty guffaw escaped Bradford, and he slapped his knee. "Aunt Muriel, I refuse to marry until I find a female as colorful as you. Life would never be dull."

"I should say not. Daventry and I had quite the adventurous life. It's in my blood, you know, and yours too, I suspect. Papa rode his stallion right into a church and actually snatched Mama onto his lap moments before she was forced to marry an abusive lecher. The scandal, they say, was utterly delicious." The duchess sniffed, a put-upon expression on her lined face. "Dull indeed. *Hmph.* Never. Why, I may have to be vexed with you the entire evening for even hinting such a preposterous thing."

"Grandpapa abducted Grandmamma? In church, no less?" Bradford dissolved into another round of hearty laughter, something he did often as evidenced by the lines near his eyes.

Unable to utter a single sensible rebuttal, Olivia swung her gaze between them. Her aunt and brother beamed, rather like two naughty imps, not at all abashed at having been caught with their mouth's full of stolen sweetmeats from the kitchen.

She wrinkled her nose and gave a dismissive flick of her wrist. "Bah. You two are completely hopeless where decorum is concerned."

"Don't mistake decorum for stodginess or pomposity, my dear." Her aunt gave a sage nod. "Neither permits a mite of fun and both make one a cantankerous boor."

Bradford snickered again, his hair, slightly too long for London, brushing his collar. "By God, if only there were more women like you."

Olivia itched to box his ears. Did he take nothing seriously?

No. Not since Philomena had died.

Olivia edged near the window once more and worried the flesh of her lower lip. Carriages continued to line up, two or three abreast. Had the entire *beau monde* turned out for the grand affair?

Botheration. Why must the Wimpletons be so well-received?

She caught site of her tense face reflected in the glass, and hastily turned away.

"And, Aunt Muriel, you're absolutely positive that Allen—that is, Mr. Wimpleton—remains unattached?"

Fiddling with her shawl's silk fringes, Olivia attempted a calming breath. No force on heaven or earth could compel her to enter the manor if Allen were betrothed or married to another. Her fragile heart, though finally mended after three years of painful healing, could bear no more anguish or regret.

If he were pledged to another, she would simply take the carriage back to Aunt Muriel's, pack her belongings, and make for Bromham Hall, Bradford's newly inherited country estate. Olivia would make a fine spinster; perhaps even take on the task of housekeeper in order to be of some use to her brother.

She would never set foot in Town again.

She dashed her aunt an impatient, sidelong peek. Why didn't Aunt Muriel answer the question?

Head to the side and eyes brimming with compassion, Aunt Muriel regarded her.

"You're certain he's not courting anyone?" Olivia pressed for the truth. "There's no one he has paid marked attention to? You must tell me, mustn't fear for my sensibilities or that I'll make a scene."

She didn't make scenes.

The *A Lady's Guide to Proper Comportment* was most emphatic in that regard.

Only the most vulgar and lowly bred indulge in histrionics or emotional displays.

Aunt Muriel shook her turbaned head firmly. The bold ostrich feather topping the hair covering jolted violently, and her diamond and emerald cushion-shaped earrings swung with the force of her movement. She adjusted her gaudily-colored shawl.

"No. No one. Not from the lack of enthusiastic mamas, and an audacious papa or two, shoving their simpering daughters beneath his nose, I can tell you. Wimpleton's considered a brilliant catch, quite dashing, and a top-sawyer, to boot." She winked wickedly again. "Why, if I were only a score of years younger ..."

"Yes? What *would* you do, Aunt Muriel?" Rubbing his jaw, Bradford grinned.

Olivia flung him a flinty-eyed glare. "Hush. Do not encourage her."

Worse than children, the two of them.

Lips pursed, Aunt Muriel ceased fussing with her skewed pendant and tapped her fingers upon her plump thigh. "I would wager a year's worth of my favorite pastries that fast Rossington chit has set her cap for him, though. Has her feline claws dug in deep, too, I fear."